D1541604

THE INVISIBLE TWINS

A NOVEL BY
TOVA SHKEDI

THE JUDAICA PRESS, INC.

THE INVISIBLE TWINS

The Twins Discovery Series — Book 1

© 2013 The Judaica Press, Inc.

ISBN: 978-1-60763-139-2

Editor: Tamar Ansh
Proofreader: Yocheved Krems
Cover and internal design and layout: Avigayil Shapiro

THE JUDAICA PRESS, INC.
123 Ditmas Avenue / Brooklyn, NY 11218
718-972-6200 / 800-972-6201
info@judaicapress.com
www.judaicapress.com

Manufactured in the United States of America

"STAY OUT OF ABBA'S WAY TODAY, kids," Sarah Abrams said as she grabbed her purse and keys from the shelf near the front door. "He's working on something important downstairs in his lab, and he asked me to remind you not to disturb him unless it's an emergency.

"Come, Ahuva'le," she continued, addressing her youngest child. "Let's get your coat; we're going to be late." She glanced at her watch, and then looked into the living room where the little girl was lying listlessly on a blanket on the hardwood floor.

Four-year-old Ahuva dragged her feet to the front door, where her mother stood waiting, and whined, "Ima, I don't want to go to the doctor.

What if he gives me a shot? Why just me? How come Elisheva doesn't have to go?" The little girl's voice was hoarse and her face was flushed with fever that a dose of Tylenol had not completely succeeded in lowering.

Sarah zipped her own coat and helped Ahuva into hers.

"Because she's not sick and you are," she replied as she tied a navy blue scarf around Ahuva's neck. "Put on your boots, please. Look at all that snow!" she exclaimed, pointing at the window, out of which they could only see a white blur. "No wonder they cancelled school today. I hope we'll make it to the doctor's office in all of this! Rafi, you're in charge, but remember, Abba is here if you absolutely need him. I hope I'll be home by lunchtime."

Waving goodbye, Sarah left, pulling a reluctant Ahuva by the hand behind her.

The door shut with a blast of frigid air and swirling flakes. Dovi, coming out of the kitchen munching on a handful of pretzels, shivered and turned to find his twin sister. Dena sat curled up on the beige sofa, her nose in a thick book, her long, straight brown hair framing her face. She didn't even seem aware that their mother had left.

Reading was Dena's favorite activity; if someone

didn't stop her, Dena was likely to spend the entire day buried in a book. As her twin, Dovi considered a large part of that responsibility to be his. He constantly had to drag her away from her reading in order to have some fun. Dovi found it curious that Dena did not often appear to appreciate his efforts.

"Dena, want to play Monopoly with me?" he asked now, determined not to let her spend their unexpected vacation perusing a book with such an obscure title as *Potential and Kinetic Energy.*

No answer.

"Dena … Dena …" he called again. "Hey, can you hear me?" Dovi finally demanded, sticking his hand in front of her face.

"I hear you." For some reason Dovi couldn't fathom, Dena sounded a little annoyed. "I'm busy right now; play with Rafi." Dena returned to her book, having barely looked up.

Their older brother was seated at the dining room table with an open math book. Dovi couldn't believe it. Were they both going to spend the day studying? They might as well be in school!

"I can't play with you right now either. I have to study for my math midterm. This stuff makes no sense to me, and I really need a good grade on this test to bring up my grade average. Play with

Elisheva," Rafi broke in before Dovi had a chance to ask.

Elisheva looked up hopefully from her coloring book and crayons, but Dovi protested, "I can't play Monopoly with Elisheva! She's too young to play."

"I am *not* too young!" Elisheva retorted, shaking her head and sending her thick black ponytail swinging. The older kids were always saying she was too little to play with them, which really irritated her. "I know how to play Monopoly just fine," she informed her brother.

"The game says age eight and up," Dovi informed her, pointing to the words on the box. "You're seven. That means you're too young."

"Ima plays with me. She doesn't think I'm too young. And Abba says it's good to play because I learn to do math." In her mind this settled the matter. After all, in her opinion, Abba was the smartest man in the whole world.

At the mention of math, Dena finally took her attention away from her book to ask Rafi, "What kind of math are you studying?"

Despite the fact that Dena, at ten, was three years younger than Rafi, she could easily keep up with his math homework. Dena was extremely gifted in almost every subject, but math was her special favorite. She seemed to have an almost intuitive understanding of the relationship between numbers.

"I'm studying geometry," Rafi answered Dena's question, taking off his black-rimmed, wire glasses and rubbing his eyes the same way his father did when contemplating a difficult problem. "It's not going so well."

Rafi's math midterm should have been that afternoon, but because school had been cancelled he was getting an extra day. A good thing, too; Rafi was a solid student but math wasn't his easiest subject; he preferred Gemara. A last-minute study session with Abba would definitely help him.

Hopefully Abba would have time tonight.

Sometimes Rafi felt he had trouble competing for his father's attention. So often these days, Abba's focus seemed to be down in his lab. He knew that Abba was working very hard to meet deadlines and commitments, but at times it was hard not to feel resentful and jealous.

First there was Dovi. It was impossible for him to be in a room without everyone knowing it, since a hurricane of chaos often seemed to follow in his wake. But people always wanted to be around him anyway. Dovi may not have been a great student, but he was so likeable that it barely seemed to matter.

And then there was Dena. Brilliant, mature, self-disciplined, she and their father could have conversations that left Rafi wondering what language they were speaking. It gave the two of them a very special bond. A bond that should have belonged to him, as the oldest son.

But he was just Rafi. There was nothing special or unique about him. Nothing to make a busy father take notice. Rafi wasn't quiet, but he wasn't loud. He was a good student, but not remarkable. He rarely made trouble, but he never did anything noteworthy either.

Rafi sighed inwardly. It was hard not to feel overshadowed by the twins.

"Can't Abba help you?" Elisheva asked, mirroring his thoughts. "He's the best in the world at math."

"Abba was going to help me," Rafi admitted, "but then he got busy with that emergency in his lab and he didn't have time. I'm not sure he even remembered."

Dena glanced quickly at Rafi, noting a strange quality to his tone.

"Yeah, I wonder what that emergency was all about," Dovi, distracted from his plans to play Monopoly, remarked before Dena could say anything. "Abba seemed pretty stressed at dinner last night. He hardly said anything."

Dena joined Rafi at the dining room table and peered into his geometry book.

"You know Abba," Dena said in an appeasing voice. "Every time he gets a new idea about 'The Machine' in his lab he forgets about everything else." She intuitively sensed the hurt that Rafi would never verbalize and wanted to mitigate it.

"He's been working on that machine for almost three years. Don't you suppose he'll ever finish with it?" Dovi asked as his sister began erasing one of the math problems Rafi had already completed.

"Even if he finished, he would just move on to the next project," Rafi answered. "That is his job after all. But this time I think his emergency is real. I overheard him telling Ima something about losing funding because the project is taking so long.

"Hey!" he suddenly noticed what Dena was doing. "I already finished that equation!"

"Yeah, but you got it wrong," Dena said matter-of-factly.

Rafi groaned, but didn't bother to argue. If Dena said it was wrong, then it was wrong. He just sighed and pushed the paper back to his sister. "Erase all the wrong ones, then," he requested.

"What does 'losing funding' mean?" Elisheva wanted to know.

"It means that the people paying Abba money to build this machine want to stop paying him. They want him to say it won't work and give up." Rafi explained.

"What does Abba's machine do?" Elisheva left her coloring and joined her older siblings at the dining room table, eager to take part in this very grown-up conversation.

"Abba never says exactly." Rafi answered. "He says it has to be kept a secret so other people don't steal his idea."

Dena was listening carefully to the conversation, even as she methodically worked through the math problem.

"It has something to do with matter and energy," she said slowly, as though unsure how much to reveal. "You know, matter is the stuff that everything is made of: atoms, molecules, things like that. Energy is something you can't touch but it powers things like machines and our bodies, which use different kinds of energy in order to work. From what I understand, Abba is trying to figure out a way to change physical things into energy and back again."

The others stared at her. "How do you know

all that?" Dovi asked her, somewhat awed.

"Some of it I heard from Abba. The rest I read," she replied simply. "It's all very interesting so I researched it a little bit. I asked Abba if I can work with him on his project but he said no. Not till I'm grown up, at least, and he hopes to have it finished long before then," Dena finished sadly.

It was hard sometimes for Dena to have her brain be so much older than her chronological years. It prevented people from really taking her seriously. And Dena really wanted to be taken seriously.

Dena identified with her father as a scientist, and Abba was gratified with her interest in his field. He enjoyed having someone in the house who could share his enthusiasm for science. For her part, Dena looked up to her father immensely and strived to be just like Abba in every way she could.

Sometimes her mother tried to interest her in history; after all, Ima was a history teacher. But to Dena, science was all about the future, all about pushing the boundaries of human knowledge and understanding the world around them. History, things of the past, just couldn't compete for her attention.

Dovi shook his head in amazement. "You are unbelievable sometimes," he informed his twin.

He also found Abba's projects interesting, and

the lab was definitely a fascinating place, but in his opinion, that kind of occupation was for adults, not kids. Apparently Abba agreed, if he wouldn't let Dena work with him.

"So Abba is basically trying to make things disappear and he hasn't yet figured out how, and now he's running out of time," Dovi summed up. "Poor Abba. I wonder if there's some way we can help him. I want to see that machine."

Dovi had a big heart and hated to see his father so worried. Although Dovi had a much greater penchant for mischief than for science, he did genuinely want to help his father. If a science experiment was exciting enough, it didn't have to be considered work. Dovi thought it might be cool to make things vanish into thin air.

Dena pushed her hair away from her face and regarded her brother. "Disappear and come back again, I think, and that's kind of an oversimplification, Abba said. And we're not allowed in Abba's lab, Dovi," she cautioned her brother, all too familiar with his propensity for rash behavior. "You know you tend to get into trouble when you don't think things through."

"And you think too much," Dovi retorted, flaring up at once.

Before this old argument could escalate, Rafi interjected.

"That's not how my teacher showed us!" He pointed at the math problem Dena had just completed. "She said we have to use this formula." He jabbed the page in his book with his finger.

"It's the right answer, isn't it?" Dena defended her work. Rafi checked the back of his book.

"Yes, but I have to show my work. I have to use the method the teacher uses! Otherwise, she takes off points," Rafi tried to explain. Ignoring this, Dena began to explain how she solved the problem. Rafi sighed and listened. Dena might be a genius, but there were some things she just couldn't understand. He knew from experience that there was no point in arguing with her.

2

DR. CHAIM ABRAMS HELD A PH.D. in applied physics and another in engineering. He had an IQ of 166 and twenty years of experience working with cutting-edge technology, but right now it all seemed to amount to nothing. He held his chin in his hands as he stared morosely at the equations on the computer screen. Something just didn't add up. Why wouldn't it work? Where was he going wrong?

For the past three years Chaim and his team had painstakingly pored over mathematical formulas, built intricate test models, and ran detailed simulations. They had made so much progress, learned so much along the way, and he felt they were so close to the answer. But that was the problem; they had been *close* to an answer, but did not *have* an answer, for months now.

The phone rang. For a moment Chaim considered ignoring it but his sense of responsibility overcame him and he answered.

"Hello, Jeff, how are you? ... A meeting? Now? I was just going over some things in the lab. Do you know what this is about?"

"Come on, Chaim," Chaim's partner, Jeff Schwartz, a brilliant mathematician, said reprovingly. "You know the boss wants to scrap the project because our progress has completely stalled. He called a meeting because he wants us to show the big money guys whatever we have to date. Since our report won't be any different than it was a month ago, he'll make a pitch for calling the matter-energy converter an unfortunate and expensive failure and turn our attention to that microwave project." Jeff sounded despondent.

Chaim's brow furrowed. "We can't give up now, Jeff; you know that. We've put too much into this. It has too much potential. We need to hang on until we make the breakthrough we've been trying for."

"Look, Chaim, maybe it *is* impossible. Maybe this project was doomed before it began. Maybe we just need to admit it." Jeff began, but Chaim interrupted him before he could continue with that line of thinking.

"I don't believe that," Chaim said flatly. "I don't believe we've come this far and can't finish."

"Alright, alright, I guess I don't either," Jeff conceded. "But now we have to convince the others. So get on over here."

"I'll try to be there in about fifteen minutes. It might take a bit longer, though, because the weather is really awful." Chaim hung up and gathered some papers into a folder. He hurried out, shutting the lab door behind him.

He gave a momentary thought to letting the kids know he was leaving, but a quick glance at his watch convinced him he would never make the meeting on time if he did. Rafi was a responsible boy; if something came up he would work it out on his own.

Besides, he reassured himself, *what could possibly happen to four kids cooped up in a house in the middle of a blizzard?* He got into the car, rubbing his hands together and shivering as he waited for it to warm up.

The kids will be fine, he thought to himself. *It's this project's future I need to be worried about right now.*

He drove carefully through the heavy snow, occasionally feeling the tires slide beneath him as he did his best to control the vehicle. He drove slowly, keeping an anxious eye on the clock.

I was crazy to come out in this kind of weather, he scolded himself, *but Jeff is right. I have to be at this meeting.*

Chaim had been in charge of this project from day one; in fact the entire thing had been his idea. He had supervised every aspect of its creation and construction with painful attention to detail. It was only right that he should be there now to argue for its continued existence.

The car emitted an ominous groan. Steam rose from its hood in billowing wisps, merging with the swirling snow. Sarah Abrams pulled over to the side of the road and nervously shut off the engine.

Maybe the car is overheating. I should let it rest for a minute, she thought.

When she tried to restart the car, the engine sputtered and died. She tried again, more desperately, but the engine would not catch. The car wouldn't start.

"Why did we stop, Ima?" Ahuva asked from the backseat of the minivan. "Are we home already?"

"No, sweetie," her mother answered. "The car

is broken. We need someone to come fix it."

She pulled her cell phone out of her purse and dialed her husband's number. It rang and rang and finally went to voicemail.

"Hello, this is Chaim Abrams. I am unable to answer the phone right now. Please leave a message and I will return your call."

Sarah hung up, and dialed again. Still no response. The third time, she left a message.

"Chaim, it's me, Sarah. I really need you to answer the phone. Please call me back right away."

She shut the phone and heaved a deep sigh. Her breath rose in front of her and cold air burned her lungs. Without the heat on, the car was getting cold, fast.

"Ima, I wanna go home already. My throat hurts and my head hurts," Ahuva complained. "And my nose is cold and my fingers are cold and my toes are cold," she continued to list her ailments.

"I know," her mother answered. "We'll get home as soon as we can. Try to rest in the meantime."

She opened her phone again to call a tow truck.

"Lady, in this weather?" was the response. "Sure, we'll send a truck. But we're overloaded with calls. Don't expect the truck to be there any time soon."

Knowing she didn't have much of a choice,

Sarah agreed to wait. She tried turning on the car again, but nothing happened.

"Let's look on the bright side," she said out loud. "Maybe this is for the best. Maybe if we had kept driving we would have been in an accident, *chas v'shalom*. There must be two feet of snow on the ground."

"My *morah* told us about that," Ahuva commented sleepily, distracted from her complaints. "It's called '*gam zu l'tovah*.' It's a story about a man who said Hashem always does good things even though everyone thought they were bad."

"I can see you paid close attention when your *morah* was reading the story," Sarah complimented her daughter, keeping her tone light. She didn't want Ahuva to see how worried she was getting. Chaim wasn't answering his phone, the car was getting colder by the minute, and who knew how long they would have to wait for a tow truck.

"Maybe I should go outside and try to stop a passing car and see if someone will give us a ride home," Sarah suggested after a few minutes of silence.

She opened her car door but the blast of frigid wind and the blinding snow drove her back into the car. She hastily pulled the door shut.

19

"It's too cold to wait outside," Ahuva noted.

"I guess so," her mother reluctantly agreed. "I guess we'll just have to sit patiently and wait."

But the car was really cold now. Sarah covered a shivering Ahuva with a spare blanket that they always kept in the car and blew on her numb fingers to try to warm them.

"I'm afraid it's not safe for us to wait too much longer. I'll try to call a taxi and see if one will come."

She hadn't brought money for a taxi, but this was turning into an emergency. However, the taxi dispatcher flatly refused to send a car.

"The roads are too bad. I can't send my drivers out in this," he told her apologetically.

Sarah shook her head in dismay.

"I'll try the house," she decided. "Maybe the kids will get Abba to answer the phone."

This is my last option, she thought. *If they don't answer, I don't know what we'll do.*

She started dialing, murmuring a silent prayer of hope.

3

ELISHEVA PUSHED AWAY HER COLORING BOOK with a restless feeling. She got up and wandered from room to room, looking for something to do. The house felt too empty without Ima home.

"Rafi, when will Ima get home? She's been gone for *sooo* long," Elisheva tugged on Rafi's sleeve to get his attention. "And I'm hungry."

And bored, she thought to herself. She didn't understand why Dovi and Rafi were so excited that there was no school today. She would much rather be with all her friends than sitting at home with nothing to do. And this morning she didn't even have Ahuva to play with.

Rafi glanced up at the clock. "She's only been

gone a little more than an hour. Go get yourself a snack if you're hungry." He had decided to take a much needed break from his math and was now sprawled on the living room floor with his miniature magnetic chess set, Dena opposite him.

As Elisheva moved off, looking despondent, Rafi examined the chessboard. It rankled him that he usually lost to his ten-year-old sister and he was determined that this time there would be a different outcome. It wasn't fair that Dena was so smart. She could see three or four moves ahead and hold several possible strategies in her mind at once.

Rafi suddenly spotted a possible move. He moved his knight and said triumphantly, "Check!"

Dena studied the board herself with a small frown on her face. "Are you sure that move is legal?"

"Why shouldn't it be?" Rafi demanded. "Are you worried that I'll win? There's nothing wrong with that move."

Dena continued to inspect the board, muttering to herself. Rafi waited for her to move with mounting impatience.

"Your turn," he reminded her.

"I know," Dena retorted testily. "Give me a minute."

She realized she was in a fix and she didn't like

it. There were just some things Dena wasn't used to losing, and chess was one of them. But Rafi was playing really well today.

She tentatively lifted her king to move when Elisheva interrupted.

"Dena, can you help me get a snack?"

"She's finally about to move," Rafi complained. "Can't you get it yourself?"

"I'm not allowed to use the knife."

Dena put her king back where it had been.

"I'll be right back," she assured her brother. She got up to go with Elisheva, privately glad for the respite. Rafi was getting better at the game. She could use a few extra minutes to review her game plan.

The phone rang.

"I'll get it!" Dovi called from the playroom. "Hello?"

"Dovi?" Ima's voice sounded frazzled. "The car broke down. I called a tow truck but Ahuva has strep throat and we're freezing here. I need Abba to come pick us up and he's not answering his cell phone. We're at the corner of Park St. and Woodmere. Tell him to come right away. Do you understand?"

"Yes," Dovi assured her. "I'll go tell him."

Dovi put down the phone and ran to the basement door. Abba's lab was down there, a wonderland of technology, computers, models, and half-completed experiments, with dry erase boards constantly covered with indecipherable letters and numbers. In general, the children were not allowed in the lab, but now Dovi felt he had a valid reason to enter.

He knocked on the door and waited, but he heard no response. Tentatively, he tried the handle and turned it. The door wasn't locked! How could that be? Abba always locked the door so he wouldn't be disturbed while he was working. He must have been even more distracted than he had seemed. Dovi went down the stairs and looked around.

"Abba?" he called. But he could see right away that the lab was empty. Abba wasn't there. *He must have left through the other door*, Dovi thought, looking at the exit that led directly to the outside.

The lab was one large room. In the center were several computers set up in a semi-circle. Surrounding them were tables with models in various stages of completion. Along the back wall were shelves with books and dozens of boxes labeled with different tools and materials. An open doorway led to a storage room filled with metals, spare computer parts, and other items Dovi couldn't begin to identify. The other walls of the lab were filled with white boards covered with handwriting, not all his father's. In front of them were desks containing paper documents with more indecipherable symbols and formulas.

Seeing his father was not present, Dovi turned to go back upstairs when a pulsing red light in the center of the computer circle caught his attention. Ignoring the warning voice in his head, a voice that sounded suspiciously like Dena, a voice that said his curiosity frequently got him into trouble, Dovi went over to the table to get a better look. What was this?

It looked like some sort of elaborate camera mounted on a cylindrical contraption of metal rods, wires, and plugs and attached to three of the computers. Only one computer appeared to be on and the screen showed a diagram of the camera machine followed by several mathematical symbols. On the side of the camera were several buttons and dials and levers. Could this be the mysterious machine Abba kept referring to?

Dovi experimentally turned a dial then pressed a few buttons, just to see if anything would happen. The red light began pulsing faster and the machine started to beep. Startled, Dovi quickly turned the dial back, but the pulsing light and the beeping only got faster. He shouldn't have touched anything, he knew. Abba would be very angry if Dovi had interfered with his work.

Dovi turned and ran back up the stairs, his mother's message completely forgotten. He found Dena in the kitchen with Elisheva, both of them munching on apple slices.

"Rafi won the game!" Elisheva was saying gleefully.

Elisheva personally felt like it was good for Dena to lose every once in a while. Though Dovi would never have admitted it, there were times when he agreed.

"I'll win next time," Dena declared in response, her tone determined. "Wait and see."

Before Elisheva could answer, Dovi barged in.

"Dena, come with me!" he exclaimed excitedly. "I want to show you something. I need your help with fixing something." He beckoned impatiently for her to follow him.

Dena regarded him calmly. Sometimes it was hard to believe she and Dovi were related, much less twins. Dovi was as excitable as she was calm, as impulsive as she was cautious, as careless as she was thoughtful. They didn't even resemble each other, Dena with her dark hair and eyes and slender form, and Dovi with his lighter features and robust build.

As often as Dovi got into trouble, Dena was there to get him out of it. She sighed. She had plenty of practice getting Dovi out of trouble.

"What is it?" she asked him.

"It's in Abba's lab. Come with me and I'll show you," he answered impatiently, as Dena set the rest of her apple slices on a plate in front of Elisheva.

Dena stared at him in alarm. "You went down into Abba's lab? Why?"

"Ima asked me to," Dovi said, briefly remembering why his mother had sent him. "I saw this machine down there, it looked really interesting. I think it's that energy machine you were talking about."

"I've already seen it," Dena said. "Abba showed it to me two days ago. Just a quick look, because I begged him."

She glanced at him, hoping this wouldn't make him feel bad, but she didn't need to worry. Dovi realized that Dena was the one who shared their father's passion for science while he preferred playing ball with his friends and building clubhouses in their big, sprawling backyard. The tediousness of the scientific process was too dull for his impetuous nature. He needed to be moving all the time; he needed excitement and activity.

The twins were very different, but they were

never really jealous of each other. In fact their personalities complemented each other quite well. Each was strong where the other was weak and they knew it. They might not always get along, but they would always help where the other needed, if they could.

Far from being upset that Dena had seen their father's secret machine while he hadn't, Dovi exhaled in relief.

"You've seen it?" he repeated. "Great, then you can fix it."

Dena frowned. "We've already been through this. Abba doesn't need or want our help with this. Just leave it alone."

"You don't understand." Dovi interrupted quickly. "You need to fix it because I kind of messed with it and now I can't get it back to the way it was. If you've seen it you can return all the settings to where they're supposed to go," Dovi explained hopefully. They both knew Dena remembered everything she saw. She had what Abba and Ima called a 'photographic memory.' "But hurry, I'm supposed to give Abba a message and he's not home," he added, Ima's phone call once again flitting briefly into his mind.

Dena shook her head in exasperation. "I can't believe you played with it! What were you thinking?"

Dovi frowned, not enjoying being reprimanded by his little sister. And she was his little sister, even if it was only by a few minutes.

"That doesn't matter now. I just did, okay? Can you fix it or not?" His guilty feelings were making him sound irritable. Trying for a more diplomatic tone, he added, "Please?"

Dena sighed with exasperation, while Elisheva's wide eyes went back and forth between them.

When will Dovi learn not to be so impulsive? Dena wondered, though she didn't say it out loud. She sensed how irritated Dovi got lately when she reprimanded him for his thoughtlessness. She couldn't figure out why it bothered him so much; she was only trying to help. She had asked her mother about it and Ima had figured that Dena better leave the scolding to their parents.

"Fine," Dena finally relented to Dovi's urging. "Let's go try to put it right."

Suddenly she had an idea.

"But if I do this for you, you owe me a favor. You know how I told you everyone in my class has to sell ten fruit trays for Tu B'Shvat as a school fundraiser? You have to sell nine of them for me. Abba and Ima will buy the tenth."

Dena was shy and reticent, and had a hard time

cold-calling strangers; going door to door selling something was even worse.

"Deal," Dovi quickly agreed.

He could probably have them all sold in an hour. He had the gift of persuasion; people tended to do what Dovi wanted them to. Dovi had a quality about him that made others want to please him.

The twins returned to the basement together. By this time the beeping had changed to one continuous whine. The light was flashing so quickly that the children had to shield their eyes. As they approached the machine, Dovi could now detect a powerful heat emanating from the camera-like contraption.

"What did you do? What did you touch?" Dena called over the noise.

"This dial here, and these buttons," Dovi called back, pointing, the other hand held protectively over his face.

Dena studied them for a moment, and then began fiddling with the controls. "I'm not sure I know what I'm doing," she admitted, "but this is how the controls were set the last time I saw them."

The whine was starting to fade. Thankfully, so was the heat. Dovi breathed a sigh of relief. He had known his sister could fix it. Their father never needed to know.

"You did it," Dovi congratulated her. "Now let's get out of here."

Dena started to go with him, but then she stopped and glanced over at the computer screen. The display had changed with the adjustments she had made. She looked at them more closely, then suddenly frowned.

"That's not right," she murmured half to herself.

"What?" Dovi questioned nervously.

She pointed at the equation on the screen. "It's not right. It's not balanced. The two sides of the equation are supposed to be equal, but these aren't. If you use the equation $E = MC^2$ then these numbers should be here, like this."

She started pressing keys.

"Wait," Dovi started, "Are you sure you should ..." But he didn't get a chance to finish. Dena input the data and pressed enter. The machine started to go into overdrive again, the mechanical whine changing to an ear-piercing scream and the blazing red glare building to such an intensity that the children could see nothing else. The temperature climbed alarmingly. Even as they both covered their faces with their hands, Dovi shouted, "Change it back!"

He wiped his dripping forehead on his sleeve. It must have been at least a hundred degrees and the temperature seemed to be still rising. The heat was making it difficult to breathe.

"I can't!" Dena cried. "I can't see!" The light was blinding and the heat was making her dizzy. She tried to stumble forward, but her feet seemed rooted to the spot where she stood.

"Let's get out of here before that machine explodes!" Dovi grabbed her hand but before they could try to move, one more big flash of light surrounded them. It was so powerful it seemed to enter their very beings. They felt the heat burning them like a million pinpricks all over their skin. Then the computer went dead with a shower of sparks and the sound of a small explosion.

The red light faded. The noise ended abruptly and the room began to cool. The uniquely acrid scent of burning circuitry filled the lab and wisps of smoke rose gently from the machinery on the table.

The twins stood motionless together in the suddenly silent basement.

"... So, the problem we've been having with the matter-energy converter, or MEC for short, is controlling the flow of power when the equation is balanced. In the simulations it works though, and I'm convinced that with a little more time we'll work out the bugs in the practical application tests."

Chaim finished his presentation and looked around the long mahogany conference table, trying to gauge the reactions of his audience. At the table sat a mix of colleagues, physicists and engineers, and their sponsors, "The Men with the Money," as he and Jeff privately called them.

Jeff spoke up now, his deep voice confident and persuasive.

"A large part of the problem now is designing a material that would be strong enough to contain the energy. We currently have several formulas to work with. We're confident that one of them will be effective and we can move on to the next phase."

This has to go well, Chaim thought to himself. *Months of hard work depend on it.*

Mr. Mark, Chaim's boss and the founder of the company, also looked around the table.

"Are there any questions for Dr. Abrams or Dr. Schwartz?" His tone was neutral, but Chaim wasn't fooled. He well remembered what Jeff had said. Mr. Mark no longer considered the MEC project to be viable.

A well-dressed, elderly man nodded in acknowledgement. Chaim recognized him as Dan Cole, one of the wealthiest supporters of Mark Technologies, Inc., the company Chaim worked for.

"You mentioned 'practical application,'" he said to Chaim. "What practical applications did you have in mind?"

"Well, for now we wanted only to change a small amount of matter into energy, just to know we can. But future practical uses for this technology would range from being able to change garbage into energy that can be put to various uses, thereby reducing the vast amounts of waste this country produces and providing a new clean source of energy, to storing sensitive equipment in a safe and secure way for transport." Chaim reminded himself to keep his explanations short and simple. Mr. Cole was a shrewd entrepreneur, but he was no scientist.

There were murmurs of approval around the table. Chaim felt a glimmer of hope. He endured these meetings because Mr. Mark insisted he attend, but he didn't enjoy them. He would much rather be holed up in the lab with his computers and models, but without financial backing he would have no lab to work in.

Mr. Mark stood up to draw the attention back to himself.

"The idea was good in theory. But obviously it doesn't work, at least not —" He broke off at the sound of a cell phone buzzing.

Chaim removed his phone from his front shirt pocket and glanced at it. His wife's cell phone number showed up on the caller ID. He saw that she had tried to call three times already. He frowned, remembering she was taking Ahuva to the doctor.

"Dr. Abrams, is everything alright?"

Chaim realized everyone was looking at him. With a mental effort he put the phone down on the table, face up.

"Yes, sorry. You were saying?" he asked, trying to return his attention to the proceedings.

Mr. Mark continued. "I think it's time to move on. This MEC doesn't have to be a total waste. Some of the work can be put toward refining —" Again the phone buzzed. This time a flicker of annoyance crossed Mr. Mark's face.

"Are you quite sure you're with us, Dr. Abrams?" Mr. Mark asked in an overly polite voice, as Chaim checked his phone again.

"I'm so sorry," Chaim apologized. "It's my wife. She wouldn't be calling again if it wasn't important. Will you all excuse me, please?"

Heads nodded as Chaim got up and left the conference room.

Why now? he thought. *I was just making my point. Now Mark will convince them that MEC can never succeed. I just hope Jeff can keep a handle on things.*

He dialed Sarah's number.

"Hi, Sarah. Sorry, I was in an important meeting. What's wrong?" He tried to keep his frustration and worry out of his voice.

"I'm sorry to disturb your meeting," his wife apologized sincerely. "It's just that the car broke down and we're stuck. I called the house and spoke to Dovi and told him to have you come pick us up. I guess if you're not home that explains why you didn't get my message. But the tow truck should be here any time now, and we're cold and Ahuva is sick and very tired. Can you please pick us up and also fill Ahuva's antibiotic prescription?"

Sarah felt bad for interrupting her husband's conference. She knew how concerned he was over the funding for his project. But there was no choice right now.

"Okay, I'm coming." Chaim reassured her, resigned. "Just tell me where you are and give me a few minutes to wrap things up here. I'll be there as soon as I can."

Chaim got the information from his wife and hung up. Returning to the conference room, he saw that the conversation had taken a decidedly argumentative turn.

"... regarding the bottom line," Jeff was saying heatedly. Jeff was a big man and he used his size to make his point, as he stood leaning over the conference table, towering over the others in the room. "There are still things we haven't tried!"

"By this point the microwave project would practically build itself," Mr. Mark insisted, his normally pallid face flushed with the heat of the debate.

"We have almost all the science for it worked out. It would really just be a matter of building a working prototype."

Mrs. Sharon, a middle-age woman in charge of the corporation's budgets, added, "The idea now is to produce something that can be sold, and quickly, so we can recoup lost finances."

"I second that," Mr. Morgan, another wealthy investor, supported her.

Joey, a fellow engineer on the team, objected. "The microwave project will still be there next month —" He broke off as Chaim raised his hand for attention.

"I'm sorry, I need to leave now to take care of something," he said. "You all know my opinion. I ask you to let us see the MEC through to the end. I guarantee that you won't be sorry."

There's nothing left to say, he thought as he made his way to the car through the heavy snow that was still falling. *They'll either approve support for the project or they won't. I've done all I can.*

"What happened?" Dovi whispered, shaken and afraid to move. "What did we do?"

He shivered as the sweat cooled on his body,

chilling him. And before, it had been so hot!

"Something terrible," Dena moaned, slowly removing her hands from her face, as though afraid to face the destruction that they had wrought. "We broke it! The project Abba's been working on for so long! The whole computer shorted out. How are we ever going to explain this to Abba? This is all your fault!" she accused Dovi. Dena was scared. She always avoided getting into trouble; how had she gotten into this?

"My fault!" Dovi exclaimed indignantly. "Who asked you to equalize that equation, or whatever it was you did? You should have just left it alone and asked Abba about it when he got home. I say this is your fault!"

"I wouldn't have even been down here if it wasn't for you," she returned. "Why did I listen to you? How do you always drag me into your messes?" She watched the computer, which continued to shoot out sparks every few seconds.

"I didn't drag you; we made a deal," Dovi reminded her. "And it's not my fault I get curious. Ima says curious people learn more."

The two looked at each other. With such different personalities, it wasn't surprising that they disagreed often. But they couldn't stay angry at each other for long. Whatever happened, they were always a pair, a team. They had started out together. It couldn't be any other way.

"This isn't getting us anywhere. We need to figure out what to do now," Dena finally decided. Her initial panic was fading and her logical thinking returning. "Maybe we can fix the computer we broke, or maybe switch everything to one of the other computers."

Dovi shook his head dubiously.

"Now you know how to fix broken computers? And look around. It's not just the computer. I think we caused a blackout. There are no lights. Face it, we're out of our league here. I think we should just tell Abba what we did and apologize. If we try to fix things again we might just make them worse. I think we've done enough damage for one day."

Dena blinked, surprised by this unusually mature attitude in her brother. But she couldn't really disagree with him. She didn't know how to fix the problems they had caused. She was usually good at coming up with answers; she was almost never the cause of the trouble.

Why did I have to touch that computer? she berated herself. Dovi was right. She had fixed his meddling. Everything would be fine now if she had left well enough alone. *What got into me?* she wondered.

"I guess you're right," she answered Dovi. Then something occurred to her. "Maybe we didn't cause the blackout. Maybe the snowstorm did."

"At the exact same time we meddled with Abba's energy machine?" Dovi questioned doubtfully. "That's an awfully big coincidence."

"Yeah, I guess you're right. Well, maybe when Ima gets home —" Dena began, but Dovi suddenly interrupted her with an exclamation of dismay. "What is it?" she asked.

"Ima! She called to say she got stuck and Abba should come. That's why I came down here in the first place. How long has it been anyway?"

Suddenly Dovi couldn't tell if they had been in the lab for ten minutes or two hours. His senses, which had been bombarded by light and sound and heat, were still reeling. "Let's get back upstairs and find Rafi. He might know what to do in case of a blackout."

Dovi began making his way toward the stairs, taking care in the darkened room. The only light came from three small windows in the back of the lab, but since the sky outside was stormy and gray and snowflakes were falling thickly, there was not much sunlight entering the basement. Dena followed slowly.

"I feel weird," she remarked, "like I'm moving through water or something." Her voice was calm, but she was starting to feel nervous about something else. What if that light was some sort of radiation that might make them sick?

"I feel that too," Dovi answered. "Probably an effect from all that light."

"You don't suppose it's dangerous, do you?" she asked, hoping for reassurance.

"Nah, I'm sure it will go away soon."

Upstairs was almost as dark as the lab. A little more light came through the larger windows, but not much. There was an unnatural stillness about the house. Dena realized she wasn't hearing the hum of the refrigerator or air from the heating vents.

"Rafi? Elisheva?" Dovi called.

No one answered, but Dena thought she heard voices coming from the living room. She headed in that direction and Dovi followed.

"Why did the lights go out? When will they go back on? Why isn't Ima back yet?" Elisheva was demanding of Rafi. She was standing by the window, holding the curtain out of the way with one hand so she could stare anxiously out into the snow. "What if something happened to her? Can't you call her?"

Rafi sighed and answered, "I tried. The phones

are down. I'm sure she's fine and it's just the snow making things take longer. And snowstorms lots of times cause blackouts. It's not really a big deal."

He tried to sound reassuring, but this was a little more than he bargained for when he agreed to babysit. He ran a hand through his dark hair, adjusted his yarmulke, and cast about for something to say to distract his little sister. "Where are Dena and Dovi?" he asked.

Elisheva shrugged. "I dunno," she answered. "They went down to Abba's lab. Dovi said something about fiddling with Abba's equipment."

"What?!" Rafi yelped. "Are you sure? But Ima said specifically to leave Abba alone today."

"I don't think Abba is there," Elisheva answered.

"Even Dovi wouldn't be silly enough to play with anything in Abba's lab while Abba isn't there," Rafi said, trying to convince himself. He got up, feeling more than just a little nervous. He knew Dovi tended to act first and deal with the consequences later. "I think I'd better go find them, just in case. Wait here," he told Elisheva.

"I want to come with you," she replied turning away from the window. The darkened house felt eerily quiet and empty and she didn't want to be left alone.

Dena decided she'd heard enough. "We're here, you don't need to find us," she said walking into the room with Dovi right behind her. "Elisheva is right, we really did mess things up, but it was an accident. We didn't mean for it to happen."

Neither Rafi nor Elisheva acknowledged her. "Fine," Rafi said to Elisheva. "You can come with me down to the lab. But don't touch anything," he warned her.

"I know, I'm not a baby," she informed him haughtily. They started to leave the room together.

Dena looked at Dovi, bewildered. Why was Rafi ignoring them?

"Rafi, don't go down to the lab," Dena said insistently. "I'm not sure it's safe. I don't know exactly what we did, but there's lots of smoke." She was thinking of the possible radiation, and how she still felt sluggish and slow.

But it was like talking to the wall. Rafi didn't even look towards her. He just walked away, Elisheva right behind him. They were heading toward the basement door.

Dovi tried to get his brother's attention.

"Look, Rafi, Ima is stuck and Ahuva has strep. Now that the phones are down how am I going to get a message to Abba? Ima needs him to pick them up."

But he was speaking to their backs. They had left him behind without even glancing in his direction.

Dovi stared at Dena and she stared back.

"We have to go stop them," Dena said, trying to ignore the tingle of alarm she felt at her siblings' strange behavior.

"He acted like we weren't there. Like he couldn't hear us, or see us!" Dovi frowned. "Why would he do that?"

He ran to catch up with Dena, who had gone after Rafi to try to stop him from going downstairs. He watched, hardly believing what he was seeing, as Dena put out her hand to catch Rafi's arm and force him to notice her. But as her fingers reached his sleeve and she grabbed it, her fingers closed on thin air. She stared at her hand and tried again. Her hand passed right through his sleeve without making contact.

"This is not possible," she croaked, astonished and horrified. In a daze, Dovi put his hand on the basement door handle. But his fingers didn't grasp it. Like Dena's, they just passed right through as if it weren't there. As Rafi opened the door and descended the stairs with Elisheva, the twins stood mutely watching.

Then Dovi spoke, all the normal traces of mischief and good humor gone from his features. "Dena, I think we have a really, really big problem."

Dena just nodded. For once, both twins were in complete agreement.

5

SARAH ABRAMS SIGHED WITH RELIEF as she sank into the front seat of her husband's car. This morning was taking way too long. Poor Ahuva was curled up miserably in the back seat, her face flushed with fever, her cold hands over her sore throat. It had been a long morning for her too.

"She's completely exhausted," she told Chaim, removing her gloves and rubbing her own hands to warm them. "I haven't been able to get ahold of the kids at home since I spoke to Dovi," she added. "I hope everything is okay there."

Chaim nodded at her words but she could tell he was distracted and not really listening. "You want to tell me about the meeting?" she offered, changing the subject to what she knew was weighing on his mind.

Chaim gave her a small smile. "They've decided something by now," he told her. "Jeff will let me know how it went."

The car skidded a little and Chaim turned his full attention to maneuvering the car over the snow-covered road.

Sarah took out her cell phone and tried to call home again. Still no answer. Chaim was concentrating on his driving so she said nothing, but she was beginning to worry. What could be going on there to keep the kids from answering the phone for the last half hour?

As soon as they pulled up in the driveway, they could see something was wrong.

"Why are all the lights out?" Sarah wondered. "Do you think they went somewhere? In this weather?"

Chaim opened the back door to get Ahuva, who had fallen asleep.

"They wouldn't do that," he assured her, lifting Ahuva out of the car. Then he smiled at his wife. "You know how we're always telling them to turn off the lights when they leave a room? Maybe they're finally listening." He carried Ahuva to the house while Sarah hurried forward to open the front door.

"Kids?" she called softly, so as not to wake Ahuva as Chaim laid her gently on the couch and covered her with a blanket. The little girl barely stirred. The house felt chilly, and Sarah shut the door quickly.

No one answered her call.

Sarah went into the kitchen. Empty. She peeked into the playroom. Also empty. "Where is everyone?" she asked out loud.

Chaim poked his head into the room. "I'm running to the pharmacy to get Ahuva's medicine," he told her. "I'll be back soon and then I'll call Jeff."

Sarah nodded distractedly, already heading upstairs to check the children's bedrooms. The house was too dark, too quiet, and too cold. A minute later Sarah's conscious mind caught up to her gut feeling and she experimentally flipped the hallway light switch up and down. Nothing.

So the power is out. Only in our house? The neighbors have lights, she realized peeking out the window at the house next door. *But more importantly, where are the kids?* The bedrooms were empty. There was really only one place left in the house to look.

No, she thought to herself, *they wouldn't. What on Earth would they be doing unsupervised in Abba's lab during a blackout?*

49

❖❖❖ ◆ ❖❖❖

"They're not down here," Rafi said unnecessarily to Elisheva. "I thought you said they came down here."

"They did," Elisheva insisted. "They must have gone back up. Maybe they're hiding."

"Why would they do that?" Rafi asked dismissively. "Do you think they fixed whatever Dovi broke?"

He glanced around, trying to figure out if something looked wrong, broken, or out of place. The smoke had dissipated enough to be only faintly detectable.

Elisheva shrugged. "Dena seemed to think she could."

Rafi didn't answer that, but privately he thought Dena figured she could do too much. He didn't underestimate Dena's intelligence but she was still only ten, after all. She didn't know everything.

"Well, we better go find them and keep them from getting into any more trouble," he said to Elisheva.

Both of them were completely unaware that the subjects of their conversation were there in the room, able to hear every word but unable to make themselves heard.

"Dena, what's happened to us? Are we dead? How come they can't see us? Why can't we touch anything?" Dovi's green eyes were wide with fear and his face was pale, so the smattering of freckles across his nose stood out clearly to Dena, even in the dim light.

Dena wished Dovi would be quiet for a few minutes so she could think. Her fear was gradually changing to curiosity and amazement. Thoughts and ideas were bouncing around her head like ping-pong balls, and all Dovi's questions were keeping her from focusing on them.

"This must be the strangest thing that's ever happened," she mused, holding up her hands and staring at them with a fascinated expression on her face.

"That's got to be something of an understatement," Dovi muttered darkly. He wished Dena would find the situation a little less interesting and a little more disturbing.

Dena ignored him. "Obviously we caused this when we tampered with the computer settings. What I'm not sure of is what we did exactly. Is this what was supposed to happen?"

"Hey," Dovi interrupted her thoughts again. "Who cares about the experiment right now, Dena?

Really! Just fix us. We'll worry about all the rest of that stuff later."

"Why do you always assume I can fix everything?" Dena demanded angrily, her dark eyes flashing. "I have no idea how to fix this. And even if that machine can undo whatever it did to us and even if I knew how to make it do that, have you noticed we can't touch anything? So what is it exactly that you think I can do?" She stood facing him with her hands on her hips.

Dovi was startled. His sister almost never lost her temper. Their mother sometimes remarked that Dena was ten going on twenty. She was the most even-tempered, unflappable person Dovi knew.

She must be more rattled than she seems, he thought, *but so am I. I'm scared. If Dena can't make this right, what will happen to us?*

It occurred to Dovi that maybe he had gotten in the habit of relying on his twin a little too much. She was always so dependable, so available for him, and putting all the responsibility on her left him free to have fun without worrying too much about the outcomes of all his little pranks and adventures. These thoughts left him feeling more than a little guilty. Dena was right; this was his fault. She would never have been in the basement if it weren't for him.

"Look, Dena, I'm sorry about all this. I never should have touched Abba's stuff. I don't know what I was thinking."

The words sounded strange to him even as he said them. Apologizing was not high on Dovi's list of favorite pastimes. Which was strange, considering that he ended up doing a lot of it. But then it was only when he was forced; no one was forcing him now.

Dena glanced at her brother in surprise, but before she could answer they heard footsteps on the stairs and a beam of light moved through the room. As one they turned to see their mother standing on the stairs holding a flashlight.

"Ima, you're home!" Elisheva cried out, running to her. She was so relieved that Ima was back. Now everything would be all right. "The lights went out, and the telephone stopped working and —"

"Yes, I realized the power went out." Sarah frowned at them. "I've been looking all over for you. You do realize this is a snowstorm and not a tornado, don't you? Why are you hiding in the basement? And where are Dena and Dovi?" Her eyes passed over the twins without seeing them.

Rafi tried to explain. "We came down here to find them. Elisheva said they were down here, but they're not."

"What would they have been doing down here? And they're not upstairs, I checked. Are you sure they didn't leave the house?" Sarah pressed, motioning with her hand for them to come up with her. "I know Dena had some fruit baskets to sell."

"I heard them," Elisheva informed her mother. "Dena was cutting an apple for us to eat and Dovi came in and said he bothered something in Abba's lab and could Dena come and put it right and then they went down." Elisheva felt very important sharing this information with her mother.

Sarah shook her head in exasperation. Dovi had always been a high-maintenance child and she was used to him making mischief, though it was usually all in good fun. But just when she thought nothing he could do could surprise her anymore, he came up with something like this!

When her husband had decided to convert their basement into his laboratory in order to spend more time at home, they had realized how important it was to make the kids understand that the lab was completely off limits. Between the expensive equipment and the delicate models, kids in the lab could do a lot of damage. Over and over again, they stressed that the lab was not for playing and no one was allowed down there without adult supervision. She couldn't believe that the twins had disregarded that rule.

The twins watched as the others went back upstairs. "We should go with them," Dovi suggested in a half-hearted voice. "We need to let them know what happened."

Dena shrugged, "We don't know ourselves what happened so how can we let anyone else know?"

But she went anyway.

I need to figure this out. The light, the energy machine, equalizing the equation … How does it all add up? I need to know more, she thought desperately. *I don't know enough.*

"I don't know enough," this time she said it out loud, her eyes desperate for reassurance that she had not made a colossal error. "I should have asked more questions. I should have read more. I should have tried harder to understand, but Abba was so secretive —"

Dovi interrupted before she could continue with her self-recriminations. "You couldn't possibly read any more than you already do; you wouldn't have time to eat or sleep if you did. Nobody expects you to know everything except you." Dovi paused to listen to himself. That had sounded rather profound, he thought. "Just answer me one thing. Are you sure we're not dead?"

"Positive," Dena replied patiently, silently thankful for his support. It eased the dread in her heart a little. "We're still in our bodies, aren't we? It's just our molecular structure that has been changed or something."

"What does that even mean?" Dovi wanted to know.

"I'm not sure," Dena admitted. "It's just something I read and it sounded good." She actually smiled a little.

"Well then, one more question," Dovi's voice turned mournful. "How are we supposed to eat? I'm starving." Dovi had an enormous appetite and it felt like hours since he last ate.

As soon as he said that, he heard Elisheva say, "Ima, is it lunchtime yet? I'm starving."

Ima glanced at the clock. "Yes, it is time for lunch, actually. But we need to find the twins before we can eat."

"But you said you looked through the whole house and didn't find them, and I'm hungry now," Elisheva complained, getting ready to battle for her rights.

"I'll go around the house again and look for them," Rafi volunteered, feeling he was partially responsible for the mishaps that had gone on while he was in charge. "You can give Elisheva lunch."

Elisheva nodded happily.

"Fine," Ima agreed. "But Ahuva is asleep in the living room. Be careful not to wake her up." She pulled a loaf of bread from the pantry and began to make sandwiches.

"I want my bread toasted," Elisheva said.

"I can't, sweetie," Ima explained. "The power is off. The toaster won't work."

Elisheva's expression turned sour. "When will the lights come back? I don't like not having power."

"I don't really like it either," Ima commiserated.

As Rafi turned to head up to check the bedrooms again, the front door opened and Abba came in with a shower of snow, holding a small paper bag, which he handed to Ima.

"Ahuva's medicine," he said, stamping his boots to remove the powdery snow. "The blizzard seems to be stopping finally. I think we got about twelve inches, on top of what we already had." His eyes fell on the flashlight in Ima's hand. "We lost power then?" he asked. "That's strange. It didn't look like any other house on the block did. How could it be just us?" He hung up his coat and blew on his cold-reddened hands.

Ima accepted the bag from him, having something

more important than the power outage to tell him. She knew he wouldn't like what she was going to say.

"Chaim, listen, when I came home I found Rafi and Elisheva in your lab," Sarah began. Chaim looked at her as she related what she knew about that morning's events, his face growing more stern by the minute.

He heard her out, then said, "I'm going down to check things out and see what they broke. I'll also see what I can do about getting power from our backup generator."

He started to leave and Sarah called after him, "Here, take this flashlight. It's darker down there than it is up here."

Chaim took the flashlight, thanked her, and went out.

Dovi felt a rock settle heavily in the pit of his stomach. He never meant to disappoint his father but it so often seemed to happen anyway. He wanted his father to be proud of him the way he was of sensible Rafi and brilliant Dena. But he was just "Dovi the troublemaker." At least once a day someone, teacher, principal, or parent, would say to him, "When will you learn to think before you act?"

Well, right now there was nothing he could do except think. Unfortunately, it was too late to help.

Rafi pushed open the door to the girls' bedroom and poked his head inside. The room was tidy and orderly; Dena wouldn't have it any other way. The yellow and white striped blankets on the bunk bed that Dena and Elisheva shared were neatly straightened but the blanket on the single bed along the opposite wall was in a crumpled heap. A siddur, tzedakah box, and a few pictures were arranged on the dresser. The closet door was closed. He could see no one in the room, but he called anyway, "Dena?" As he expected there was no answer.

He checked the room he and Dovi shared, his parents' room, and the spare room his mother used for sewing, his tension rising all the time. His parents had only recently begun trusting him with the responsibility of babysitting for his siblings. It wasn't that he enjoyed babysitting that much but Dovi's shenanigans were making him appear unreliable. After peeking into the attic, Rafi finally had to face it: the twins were nowhere to be found.

Suddenly the lights turned back on. The refrigerator began to hum and the house immediately felt livelier and warmer. Sarah looked up from the tuna salad sandwiches she was handing to Elisheva to ask Rafi if he had found the twins, but at the expression on his face she didn't bother. Clearly he wouldn't appear so glum if he had found them.

"They're not out back, I checked," she told him.

"I'm so sorry, Ima," Rafi began. "I should have —"

His mother cut him off before he could finish. "This isn't your fault," she said clearly. "You understand? The twins are not babies. They're old enough to know they should have told you if they were leaving, and they're definitely old enough to know they shouldn't have played around with Abba's things. We've told you all hundreds of times. Maybe more. This isn't your fault," she repeated. "And don't worry too much. We'll find them."

At least we have power back so we can call their

friends, she thought to herself. *Chaim must have got the backup generator working.*

As though in answer to her thoughts, Chaim came up the stairs. "Baruch Hashem, we got that generator installed when we put in the lab," he commented. "And now for the bad news. I don't know exactly what they did down there, but somehow they completely destroyed the MEC's main computer. It's fried. It's as though they sent an enormous energy surge through the machine, way more than it could hold. Burned out the circuits." He shook his head. "Have you found them yet?" He asked looking around. "I want them to show me what they did."

"No," Sarah answered, handing him a plate with two sandwiches. "They're not here. They must have gone to friends."

"Without telling anyone? In a blizzard? Are you sure?"

Sarah shook her head. "Now that the power is back I'll call some of their friends," she decided. As she reached for the telephone, however, she heard a plaintive cry from the living room.

"Ima, my throat hurts so much!" Ahuva wailed miserably.

"I'm coming to bring your medicine, sweetie," Sarah called quickly, hurrying towards her.

"Here you are," she held the little medicine cup to Ahuva's lips. "Drink this down and you'll start to feel better soon."

Ahuva turned her curly brown head away from the medicine.

"It's yucky," she asserted, "and it smells bad."

"I know," her mother sympathized. "But you really need to take it in order to feel better. It will only taste yucky for a minute and then you can drink some cold orange juice."

Ahuva reluctantly began to sip the thick pink liquid, shuddering dramatically as she did.

"There you go," Sarah encouraged her. "That wasn't so bad, was it?"

Ahuva just made a face, and reached for the cup of orange juice.

Dovi longingly eyed the remains of his mother's sandwich making and watched enviously as Rafi and Elisheva ate their lunch at the kitchen table.

"I'm starving," he moaned. He tried to take bread from the loaf on the counter, but his hands passed right through. He looked so comically mournful that Dena had to laugh at him.

"It's not funny," he huffed indignantly. People

always made fun of how much he ate. "If we can't eat, we really will starve."

Dena nodded, her mirth fading. "I'm kind of hungry too," she admitted. "But right now I'm more worried about what's going to happen when Ima tries to find us at our friends and we're not there. Do you think they'll call the police?"

Dovi shrugged, "Eventually, yeah, but it won't help. The police won't be able to find us either."

"I know that. But it will make everything messy and complicated,"

"Messy and complicated?" Dovi repeated incredulously. "I think messy and complicated came back when we realized we could walk through walls, which was only shortly after we realized no one can hear or see us."

Dena waved this away impatiently. "Yes, all that is pretty complicated; but once the police are involved Abba's project won't be a secret anymore. Other people would study it, it might be in the news, it might get taken away. Who knows?"

Dovi thought this over. "Yeah, I didn't think of that," he admitted. "We have to find a way to let Abba know we're here before he involves the police."

"Let's go back to the lab," Dena suggested. "If there's anywhere we'll be able to get through to him it will be there."

❖❖❖ ◆ ❖❖❖

Chaim was frowning over the tangle of blackened wires connecting the computer to the MEC when his cell phone buzzed.

"Hello?" he answered distractedly.

"Everything okay, Chaim?" Jeff asked. "You left an awfully important meeting quite suddenly."

"Oh, yes, Sarah took Ahuva to the doctor and the car broke down on the way home. I went to pick them up."

For the moment he couldn't bring himself to tell Jeff about the damage to the MEC. Jeff was a close family friend; had been for years. He wasn't completely *frum*, but through his association with the Abrams family over the years he had become more traditional. He was a frequent guest at their Shabbos and Yom Tov table and the kids adored him. But Jeff had no children of his own. His whole life was his job. The problems with the MEC weighed even more heavily on his mind than they did on Chaim's.

"What happened after I left?" Chaim asked anxiously.

"The board wants a demonstration of the MEC's capabilities at noon tomorrow," Jeff informed him. "Then they'll decide on the project's future."

"Tomorrow?!" Chaim repeated, alarmed. "But

the best we've been able to do is melt things down into unrecognizable masses of matter. Nothing so far has been able to handle the flow of energy. And today's blackout didn't help matters."

"What blackout?" Jeff questioned. "I didn't notice any blackout."

"We lost power," Chaim said slowly. His mind was beginning to put a few things together. They had lost power but their neighbors apparently hadn't; his main computer was a melted mess. He had assumed that somehow the blackout had caused a power surge in his computer, but what if it was the other way around? He remembered Sarah saying the twins had played with his machine. What had they done? With the computer fried he couldn't tell exactly, but he suddenly felt that it was vital that he figure it out.

"Chaim, you there?" Jeff's voice called to him over the phone.

"Yes," Chaim said quickly. "Listen, Jeff, we are just going to have to put together some type of demonstration by tomorrow. We'll work through the night if we have to."

"Want me to come over there? Two heads are better than one," Jeff volunteered.

"No," Chaim declined hastily. "We'll just be in

each other's way. I'm going to make some adjustments here and then run some more tests. You go through the numbers again. Try every variation you can think of."

"Gotcha," Jeff acquiesced agreeably. "I'll feed the numbers to you through the computer."

Chaim winced at the word "computer," but he didn't argue.

"Fine, let's see what we come up with."

He hung up and stared at his phone for a moment, rubbing his chin distractedly.

"You should have told him the truth about the damage," Sarah said from the stairs. She had come to collect his lunch plate and see if he made any progress fixing the twins' handiwork.

"I couldn't do that to him," Chaim replied wearily, removing his thick glasses and polishing the lenses. "Besides, I have an idea how to fix it."

Two invisible pairs of eyes, one green and one brown, brightened at this news but then grew concerned again at their mother's next words.

"I called all of the twins' friends that I can think of," she said worriedly. "No one has seen them. Do you think we should call the police?"

7

D<small>ENA</small> <small>GRABBED</small> D<small>OVI'S</small> <small>ARM</small>, her eyes widening in alarm. They were running out of time. Dovi ran in front of his father waving his arms and calling, "Abba! Don't call the police! We're here! We're here!"

Dena tugged him back, recognizing the futility of his efforts. A thought was tickling the edge of her mind and she was trying to bring it into focus.

Their father spoke, hearing nothing but his wife's suggestion. "Maybe we should wait a little longer. They've only been missing for about two hours. The police won't take it seriously for a while yet."

Sarah shook her head uneasily. "I just have a bad feeling that something is wrong. It doesn't make sense for them to disappear like this, no matter what they did to your equipment. And another thing; if they're not in the house — and they're not — then they left in a blizzard and two feet of accumulated snow —" She paused for effect, then finished, "— without taking coats or boots."

Chaim pondered that in silence for a moment. "Wait one more hour," he said finally. "If we haven't heard from them by then, we'll call the police."

He was well aware of what calling the police would cost his project if it was at all connected to the twins' absence. Surely there was an innocent explanation for all this! At least, he prayed there was.

Sarah understood what this project meant to her husband. She unwillingly agreed to wait one more hour and left him alone with a puzzle that was rapidly becoming extremely disturbing, if not downright ominous.

Dovi paced the length of the lab in a highly agitated state. He barely noticed that every so often his elbows or hands would pass through an object that should have been solid, as though it wasn't there.

"We're going to be stuck like this forever," Dovi

muttered to himself as he paced. "I'm never going to be able to eat again. On the other hand, I'm not going to be able to do homework again either. I wonder if it's a worthwhile tradeoff," he mused, rubbing his chin thoughtfully.

Dena would have laughed at her brother if the situation hadn't been so dire. She leaned as close as she could over her father's shoulder as he began removing all the fused plugs and wires connecting the MEC to the computer and replacing fresh wires into a new computer. The he opened the old computer and removed the memory.

"Do you think Abba can figure out what we did from the fried computer's memory?" Dena wondered excitedly. "Do you think he'll be able to tell that I equalized the equation?"

Interrupting his pacing, Dovi came over to watch Abba with her. "Dena, I still don't understand. Abba must have realized that the equation wasn't balanced. He had to have had a reason for doing that. But if the MEC wasn't working, why wouldn't Abba just balance the equation himself? Obviously we got results," he concluded dryly.

Dena considered this, and then answered slowly, "We heard Abba say something about melted messes, about too much energy. I think balancing the equation causes a flow of energy more powerful than the machine can handle. That's why the computer blew up when we tried it. And not balancing the equation doesn't allow the machine to actually work and do what it's supposed to."

"I guess getting results doesn't help much if the machine blows up every time it's used," Dovi observed.

"I don't think this is the result Abba had in mind," Dena responded. "Remember, the point is to turn matter into energy. Not to make people invisible."

Abba had removed the hard drive from the ruined computer and was contemplating it in his hands.

"I don't think Abba ever intended to use his machine on people," Dovi pointed out, and Dena conceded that this was true.

Possibly, using the machine on a person had an unintended effect. Had they been turned into energy? How could that be, if they were still alive? But that was what the machine was designed to do. It didn't add up, and Dena wasn't used to being stumped by intellectual puzzles. It wasn't really a feeling that she particularly liked.

◆◆◆ ◆ ◆◆◆

Sarah absently cleaned up from lunch, all the while keeping one eye on the clock. The minutes seemed to tick by with agonizing slowness. There must be something wrong with this clock, she kept thinking, going to peek into the living room to check the clock there. But that clock read the same way.

Chaim might be wrapped up in his difficulties with his work, but her intuition was telling her that all was not right with the twins. They were in trouble; she felt it with every fiber of her being. They needed her help and she was just sitting doing nothing. But she had promised Chaim they'd wait an hour. She would keep that promise, however difficult that was.

Meanwhile, she had dinner to prepare. Ahuva had fallen back to sleep, Elisheva was reading, and Rafi was studying again, this time for a Gemara test, and the house was too quiet.

It was never this quiet when the twins were around. Dena might constantly be buried in a book, but she had a tendency to surface every few minutes with some burning question, usually something about the nature of the universe. And Dovi was always bouncing into and out of trouble, a ball of energy, a life force running through the family. His sunny smile and witty remarks could pull anyone out of a bad mood.

Forty minutes left.

Sarah remembered when the twins were born. How she felt when she had been told there were two of them, overjoyed and overwhelmed at the same time. The twins were like two sides of a coin, perfectly balanced with each other. Everything was always okay as long as they had each other. She hoped they had each other now.

Thirty minutes left.

There would probably be school tomorrow so she should really start preparing a lesson plan. She'd be teaching Jewish history all afternoon at the girls' high school. Oh, and she needed to arrange a babysitter for Ahuva.

Twenty minutes left.

Jeff typed a few numbers into the computer, deleted some and replaced them with other symbols. He watched the results scroll across his screen, leaning forward in concentration. Jeff worked best with a deadline, and now he was focused, driven, completely determined to bend the numbers to his will, to force the laws of physics to adjust to his commands.

At the same time, however, Jeff was aware that not all was as it should be with his old friend and partner. Chaim had been too vague, too distracted, which didn't make sense. What could possibly distract Chaim from their project at this critical juncture? What could possibly be more important than the display they would be expected to give in twenty-four hours?

An alert beeped on his computer letting him know that he had received an email. Jeff checked and saw that it was from Chaim. Opening the email, Jeff read, "Run these numbers through with a balanced equation. Send me the results as soon as you have them. Thanks." There followed a list of numbers and mathematical symbols.

Jeff frowned as he traced his finger along the formula.

What is Chaim playing at? he wondered to himself, scratching his head of shaggy brown hair in confusion. *He knows as well as I do that it doesn't matter if the conversion works when the matter and energy are properly balanced since we haven't been able to get our equipment to tolerate that much energy. Even if the matter is transformed, the converter will be fried. It won't be able to store the energy and the whole thing will be pointless.*

Nevertheless, Jeff began running scenarios using the data Chaim had sent him. He ran it once, examined the results, and tweaked the numbers slightly. He input the data again, then stood up and stretched while he waited for the computer to analyze the new data. He was pouring himself a cup of coffee when the computer chimed, letting him know it had completed its calculation.

Holding the hot cup in his large hand, Jeff bent over the monitor. The information was there on the screen, just as he had expected. The high level of energy Chaim's formula had provided would overload the MEC completely. The matter-energy converter simply wouldn't be able to contain it. Shaking his head in dismay, Jeff sent the information off to Chaim and prepared to return to the drawing board. After all, he had a deadline to meet.

THE GLOW OF THE COMPUTER SCREEN reflected off Chaim's glasses as he contemplated the data Jeff sent him. The hard drive from the burned out computer had thankfully been intact. It had only taken a short time for him to install it in another computer and retrieve the data hidden inside. The key to this mystery. Energy equals matter times the speed of light squared. The balanced equation had been input into the computer and the machine activated.

Clearly this was the twins' work. Dena was the only one who would know how to play with the numbers that way and Dovi was the only one who would manage to put her in a situation where she would be tempted to do it.

But why did she turn on the converter? he pondered. She had better sense than that, and he was sure he had impressed upon her how sensitive this experiment was. Dena was not an impulsive child and she almost always did as she was told. Dovi must have been the one who turned on the MEC. It was the only explanation that made any sense.

So he knew what had happened. The flow of energy was too much for the MEC and it had burned itself out, blew itself up. It was virtually inoperable now, but Chaim knew he could fix it. This was hardly the first time something like this had occurred. Over the months of trying to perfect the technology, they had miscalculated how much energy the machine could handle a number of times.

"I know what happened to the machine," he said out loud to himself, unaware that he had an audience. "I just wonder what happened to the twins."

Shaking his head, he began his repairs.

The hour was up. Sarah had prepared vegetable soup and lasagna for dinner and arranged to drop Ahuva off at her sister Rivkie's house tomorrow afternoon. She had duly assured Rivkie that Ahuva would have received three doses of antibiotics by that time and would no longer be contagious, but the preschool wouldn't let her come back until she had been fever-free for at least twenty-four hours.

Sarah was finished waiting. She had given Chaim the hour as she had promised, but there was still no sign of the twins. It was time to call the police.

Chaim didn't argue this time. "I found out what they did in my lab," he told her, "and they sure caused quite a mess. Nothing I can't fix," he hurriedly assured her. "I thought there might be something down there to explain where they might have gone, but so far I've found nothing. So let's call."

"Ima, are Dena and Dovi ever going to come back?" Elisheva asked, overhearing her parents, her green eyes clouded with worry.

"Of course they are," her mother answered quickly. "Just as soon as we find them." She turned to Chaim. "You call."

He nodded, took the phone and tried to get out of earshot of Elisheva, but she followed him curiously. Elisheva had ears that seemed specially tuned to pick up things she wasn't supposed to hear. Although she was only in first grade, she knew more about what went on in school than Dena, in the fifth grade, did.

"Elisheva," Sarah called, trying to distract the girl. "Why don't you go play with Ahuva?"

"She's watching a video," Elisheva answered promptly, still straining to hear her father's conversation.

"So watch it with her. Or ask her if she wants to play with you. But please leave Abba alone for a few minutes." Sarah insisted.

Elisheva pouted, "It's a baby *aleph-beis* video. And she's not feeling well enough to play, she said so." But she went off to the playroom in search of her sister.

Rafi was also acutely aware of what was going on but he listened silently, keeping out of the way. In spite of his mother's words he was still feeling like this whole mess was his fault. He strained to listen and caught snatches of what his father was saying.

"... report two missing kids ... ten-year-old twins, a boy and a girl ... how long? About three hours ... I know it hasn't been very long ... No, they're not in the house; we searched the whole place from top to bottom ...." His father's voice was getting louder. "Yes ... yes, we'd really appreciate that, thank you."

Rafi couldn't help turning to look expectantly at his father as he reentered the room.

"Well?" Sarah prompted.

"As I expected, they didn't take it very seriously. They are overwhelmed right now with accidents and things because of the snowstorm. However, they said they would try to send someone as soon as they could. In the meantime, they'll let all their officers know to keep an eye out for two missing children," Chaim related.

Sarah didn't think much of this. "What are we supposed to do until then?" she demanded. After a second's thought she added, "I can go out in the car and look for them. Maybe they went to the library, or the kosher mart —" She broke off as her husband shook his head.

"The roads are really bad, according to the police. We shouldn't go out driving. And can you really see them going out to the library or store in this weather, without coats and without permission?" he asked.

Sarah had to admit that she could not. Dena was nothing if not thoughtful, and Dovi, while more impulsive, at least wasn't that insensitive to other people's feelings. The twins must know that their parents were worried about them, and they would surely let them know where they were if they could. These thoughts, far from being reassuring, only made her more worried.

Chaim seemed to follow her train of thought, for he said heavily, "For now there's nothing we can do but wait and daven for them. Hopefully wherever the twins are they are safe and warm. Come, let's say some Tehillim together now. Then I'm going back to my lab to get some work done," he added. "After all, I have that deadline of noon tomorrow."

After several minutes, Chaim closed his Tehillim and stood up.

"Please let me know when the police come."

He turned to go, but Rafi hurriedly stopped him. "Abba, what if I go out and look for them on foot? Just around the neighborhood?" He was desperate to feel useful.

Chaim considered the pale face with the intense brown eyes for a minute, but then answered, "If they were that close, why wouldn't they just come home?"

"Maybe one of them fell and got hurt or something," Rafi suggested. "Maybe they're building a snowman, or maybe they're sledding in the park and lost track of time."

"Alright," Chaim finally agreed. "But stay close and take a cell phone. And don't stay out long. If you don't find them within twenty minutes come home. Understand?"

Rafi nodded quickly, gratefully.

"And bundle up," his mother added.

Rafi put on his coat, hat, gloves, and boots, and then headed out into the cold and snow.

Dena was alone in the lab, finally able to concentrate on her situation since Dovi had gone upstairs to keep tabs on what was happening with the rest of the family. Now Dena was moving about the lab, unable to touch anything, but reading every open file, examining every dry-erase board, and scrutinizing the data on each computer screen.

A reference to thermal energy. That was heat energy, she knew, remembering the burning sensation on her skin when in the grip of the red light. *Thermodynamic energy, the energy holding particles of matter together. A machine that converts matter into energy, stores that energy, and transforms it back into matter.*

She felt that understanding was just out of her reach. Each individual fact made sense to her, but she couldn't seem to put it all together to understand the science behind the MEC the way her father did. She found this realization humbling.

I was silly to think that just because I like science

and math and am good at it that would make up for the years of study and experience that Abba has, she told herself. *I was too proud and now I'm paying for it. Dovi and I both.*

Dena recognized that she was smart, the smartest girl in her class, certainly. She never saw any point in false modesty, in pretending she wasn't gifted, but her parents had always cautioned her against being proud, or against making others jealous. She had tried to take their words to heart. Her classmates seemed to know she was always willing to help anyone who needed it with her schoolwork. Her siblings certainly knew it; she helped Dovi with his homework every other day.

But how do I make him feel about it? she wondered. Dovi never seemed bothered by the fact that she was so much better at school than he was. Actually, Ima had told them that their I.Q.s were quite similar; Dovi just didn't apply himself the way she did. He did all right in school, but he wasn't top of the class or anything. Whenever she asked him why he didn't put more effort into his schoolwork, he shrugged, acknowledging that school was important but maintaining that friends and fun were important, too.

Everything in balance, she thought to herself

now, *that's what he's always been trying to say and I never really understood.*

A textbook on one of the desks was open to a page headed *Changing Forms of Energy.* Dena tried to make out what was written but a large manila envelope carelessly tossed onto the book was making it hard to see. She tried to push the envelope away, feeling that curious tingling feeling as her hand passed through solid matter.

"I don't think I will ever get used to that feeling," she said out loud.

A visible sentence in the book caught her eye. What did it say? "The law of conservation of energy states that energy can never be created nor destroyed, merely transformed. The addition of heat energy speeds up molecular motion —" That was all she could see. She sighed with frustration. This appeared to be relevant; she again remembered the piercing heat that had assaulted them.

"What if that heat energy excited the atoms in our bodies and caused them to move at super speed? Would that make us invisible?" she wondered out loud.

She now wished Dovi was down here with her so she could use him as a sounding board. Had she figured out what had happened? How could she know if she was right? And if she was right, what then? How could they slow their atoms back down? How could they become visible again?

A sudden noise on the stairs startled Dena. She spun around, her arms flailing out as she tried to keep her balance. Her arm went through the new wires her father had just installed in the MEC, sending up a shower of sparks, and for the second time that day, filling the lab with the sharp smell of burned silicone and melted rubber.

9

CHAIM STOOD AT THE ENTRANCE to his lab and stared in disbelief at his smoking, sparking wires. How was this possible? He had just replaced those wires!

Dena also stared at the new mess she had created. She had created! She had caused a visible reaction and her father had been there to witness it! She had to let Dovi know. She spun and ran up the stairs, passing her father, calling, "Dovi! Dovi, where are you? Something amazing happened!"

He came barreling toward her and the two narrowly avoided a head-on collision.

"Whoa," Dovi put out both hands to stop her. At least she felt solid. "What happened?"

She related what had occurred when her hand

had come in contact with the live wires, and her theory about the energy exciting the particles in their bodies.

"Poor Abba," Dovi said sympathetically. "That's the second set of wires you've destroyed today."

Dena waved this away.

"Forget about the wires, that's not the point. I was able to affect a physical object, and Abba was able to see it. I think we can find some way to use this to communicate with him," Dena stressed.

Her brother nodded. "That's definitely good news. But the police are coming, and as far as Abba knows he's just having really bad luck with his wires today. How are we going to get him to associate the burned wires with us?" Dovi questioned.

"I haven't gotten that far," Dena admitted, somewhat deflated. "But at least it's something. Let's go make some more sparks. We'll get Abba's attention together!"

Exasperated, Chaim began to remove the burned wires, overcome with a feeling of déjà vu. Suddenly, he dropped the wires and jerked back as sparks once again began shooting out of the wire he had been holding. He yanked the end out of the computer terminal and watched as the sparking died away.

What is going on here? he wondered. *This isn't normal. The first set of wires, I understand; the twins shorted those out. Did the twins do something else that I'm not yet aware of? Something that might explain their mysterious disappearance? Something that's continuing to destroy my equipment?*

He wasn't sure whether that would be a good thing or not. He just couldn't buy the fact that they had run away or something. They just wouldn't do that. He knew it.

He had to make some headway on his project; a lot of people were counting on him and by wasting time he was letting them down. He felt like he wasn't able to concentrate, however. This lab had always been his haven, the place where he could come to think, to work, undisturbed by the outside world.

But now two of my kids are missing and the project just doesn't seem so important anymore. But I need to try.

He started to return to work but almost immediately stopped again turning slowly around his lab, shaking his head in puzzlement.

◆◆◆　◆　◆◆◆

"You start by the radiator, I'll go to an outlet," Dena instructed.

"Are you sure this is safe?" Dovi asked doubtfully. "Even little kids are always told to keep away from electrical outlets. I'm not sure I like the idea of sticking our hands in one."

"I'm not a hundred percent sure, but things can't really be worse than they are right now, can they?" Dena asked rhetorically.

Dovi didn't have an answer to that, but he offered, "I can take the outlet, if you want."

Dena looked up at him. "Thanks," she said, touched, "but I got us into this mess. I'll do the outlet."

Dovi moved toward the radiator. "If you're sure," he acceded. "Just say when."

"Now!" Dena cried, and she stuck her hand into the electrical outlet at the same time that Dovi plunged his entire arm into the radiator.

The reaction was immediate. Electrical energy crawled up and down her arm, blue and red sparks shooting out from the wall. The sensation was unpleasant, but not really painful, kind of itchy really. And prickly. And burning …

She jerked her arm out of the socket, breathing hard, flexing her hand. Her fingertips were slightly blackened. She glanced over at Dovi and he caught her eye. He too removed his arm and examined it. Then Dena saw her father look searchingly around the room.

"He's noticing!" Dena exclaimed excitedly. She proceeded to place her other hand in the outlet. Dovi followed suit. Their father began walking slowly around the lab, scrutinizing the radiator, examining the outlet, and scratching his beard in bafflement.

"What in the world …?" he muttered. He saw the shower of fiery light stop and started to straighten up when they began again.

He froze.

"Come on, Abba," Dena encouraged. "Put it together. Understand what we're trying to tell you." Her fingers were starting to burn again, and she yanked herself away from the outlet. As soon as she lost contact with it, the sparking stopped. A second later Dovi was also forced to remove his hand.

Holding their breath, the twins watched their father glance from the outlet to the radiator and back again. His brow furrowed, lips pursed, he ran his hands over the radiator. Of course, nothing happened. He went back to his computers and fingered the tangled pile of charred wires. Outlet, radiator, wires, all sources of electrical energy.

"He's going to understand! He's getting it, Abba's getting it!" Dovi exclaimed.

The twins stood together, their excitement mounting. If their father could just figure out what had happened to them, he would be able to fix everything.

With a frown of concentration, their father reached for his computer.

Then the peal of the doorbell echoed through the house.

Rafi trudged through a foot of snow, shivering in spite of his warm coat. Everywhere he looked, he saw nothing but white. He took a breath and the frigid air burned his lungs.

Here and there he saw abandoned cars, stuck in the mountains of snow, their owners gone to seek shelter from the cold. There was no one about. He was alone, walking up and down the streets, calling for his brother and sister.

"Dena! Dovi! Can you hear me?" he shouted, over and over again. But the wind snatched the words away as soon as they left his cold lips.

He so badly wanted to help. He wanted to be the one to find them, to prove himself worthy of his parents' trust, to have their eyes light up with pride in him. He wanted it to be his turn.

Now if he could just find the twins ….

Where could they be? he wondered, trying to think like Dovi or Dena. *The pizza place? The sledding hill? The library? Are they even together?*

He was nearly numb from cold by the time he had checked all the places on his mental list. He went to the sledding hill last, feeling his hopes rise as he spotted several bundled up figures playing together in the park.

They turned to look at Rafi as he joined them and he recognized some of Dovi's good friends.

"Hey, look, it's Dovi's brother!" one boy called out to the others, and they came and crowded around him.

"Where's Dovi?" another boy asked him. "I tried calling to see if he wanted to join us here and no one answered the phone at your house."

"We lost power," Rafi explained absently. "But it's back now. And Dovi isn't home. None of you have seen him?"

All the boys shook their heads.

"I'd have expected him to be the first one here," someone else commented.

"Do you want us to help you look?" a ruddy-faced

boy offered reluctantly, with a longing glance toward the sledding hill.

Rafi hesitated a moment, considering it, but then he shook his head.

"Thanks anyway," he declined. "But if you see him, tell him to come home," Rafi instructed them, turning to leave the park.

"And if you see him, tell him to come sledding with us," someone called after him. Rafi just waved in response, not turning around.

He was ready to resume his search, but a glance at his watch confirmed that his time limit had long since expired. Sighing, he headed for home.

10

At the sound of the bell, Sarah Abrams ran toward the door, her heart racing hopefully. Rafi had been gone considerably longer than twenty minutes, but he had thoughtfully called so she wouldn't worry about him, at least.

Opening the door, she found Rafi on the doorstep, accompanied by a tall, lanky police officer. A deep disappointment went through her when she saw that the twins were not with them.

"I didn't find them," Rafi informed her. "But Officer Tendall is here to talk to you about the twins." Rafi looked positively frozen.

"Come in," Sarah invited. They entered, and Sarah quickly shut the door against the cold.

"Ma'am," the officer greeted. "I met your son outside. He says the children you reported missing haven't been found yet?"

"No," Sarah confirmed. "They're still missing. It's been nearly four hours." She led him into the living room. "Rafi, run down to the lab and get Abba." She felt like she needed her husband with her now to help her handle this. Chaim's project was just going to have to wait until this was dealt with. "Would you please sit down?" she addressed the officer as Rafi ran off. "Would you like a hot drink?"

"Thank you, no," Tendall answered politely. He seated himself on one of the dining room chairs and removed a small spiral notebook and a pen, which he clicked to open and then held poised over the notebook.

"My husband will be just a minute, if you don't mind waiting."

The police officer nodded agreeably and leaned back in his chair.

"Abba?" Rafi called down the basement stairs. "The police finally came and Ima wants you to come up and talk to him. He's waiting for you now."

Chaim glanced toward Rafi on the stairs and then back around his lab, torn between his desire to talk to the police and get them started searching for his two missing children, and solving the mystery in his own lab. Normally there would have been no competition, but his instinct told him the strange occurrences in his lab were connected to the twins in some way. As yet he couldn't explain how, but it was certainly possible that he would do the twins more good here in his lab than upstairs talking to the police. But Sarah wanted him there with her and he knew how worried she was.

That clinched it. The mystery in his lab would wait. Determinedly putting it out of his mind to think about later, he followed Rafi to talk to the policeman.

The twins watched him go, their shoulders sagging uniformly in defeat.

"I can't believe the timing," Dena groaned. "We were so close! Abba was starting to understand, I could tell."

"Maybe," Dovi agreed. "But he'll come back to it. You know how Abba is about finding an explanation for everything. He's a scientist after all. We got him curious and that's something."

"You're right," Dena agreed, straightening up and squaring her narrow shoulders. "But for now maybe we should go hear what they're telling the police."

Chaim entered the living room and Officer Tendall stood to shake his hand. Chaim took in the officer's appearance at a glance: tall, about six foot two, thin, around forty-five to fifty years old, thick, salt-and-pepper hair, and a mustache. Intelligent grey eyes studied him, missing nothing.

"I'm Dr. Chaim Abrams," Chaim introduced himself.

"Officer David Tendall," the officer replied, reseating himself. "Maybe you can tell me what's happened."

Sarah began, explaining how she had had to take her little girl to the doctor and school had been cancelled due to the weather. "My husband was in the house, working. I left Rafi in charge." She indicated her son, adding, "He's a very dependable boy."

"How old are you, son?" Tendall asked Rafi directly.

"Thirteen," Rafi answered.

He had seated himself in a corner of the room, close enough to take in everything that was being said, but far enough not to be in the way. Ahuva and Elisheva, hearing an unfamiliar voice, edged into the room. On seeing the policeman, Ahuva immediately climbed onto her mother's lap. Elisheva stood near Rafi, her somber green eyes fixed on the policeman.

"What happened once your mother left?" Tendall continued.

Rafi explained what had happened that morning, how Dovi had answered their mother's phone call and apparently gone down to the lab. He related what Elisheva had told him had gone on in the kitchen, leading to both twins going into the basement. "And we never saw them come up, and they're not still down there," he concluded.

Tendall was taking notes in his little notepad. There was a little pause while they waited for his writing to catch up. Finally he looked up again, this time at Elisheva. "You're sure they said they were going downstairs to the lab?" he asked.

Elisheva was getting tired of everyone questioning her story but she knew the policeman was there to help and she must answer politely.

"Yes, I'm sure. Dovi said he needed help fixing something he broke and Dena said she'd help him."

"And you were no longer home?" Tendall asked Chaim.

"No, I wasn't," Chaim confirmed. "I had been called to an unexpected meeting. I left through the basement door."

"And this was how long ago?" Tendall continued.

"About four hours," Rafi responded. "When the power went out we went down to look for them and they weren't there." He indicated himself and Elisheva. "We were down there when our mother came home."

"Wait a second. 'Lost power'?" Tendall looked up, frowning. "There were no reported power outages in this area."

Chaim cleared his throat. Now they were going to get into sensitive territory. He wasn't sure how much he wanted to say about his work — he was afraid the police would want to pry into things he couldn't share. If it would help the twins, he would hand over the very schematics to the project, but he just didn't believe that it would help.

"I think the twins caused a very large electrical surge in some equipment I was working on in my lab and that's why we lost power," Chaim said carefully. "Nothing to do with the weather."

Officer Tendall studied him for a moment and then reviewed his notes. "Is it possible they ran away when they realized how much mischief they caused?"

Chaim and Sarah exchanged glances. "We wouldn't have thought so," Sarah answered, "but we aren't absolutely sure, of course. Anything is possible. We can't understand, however, how they could possibly leave in this weather without at least taking coats."

Tendall considered this thoughtfully. "Could someone have entered the house without your knowledge?" he asked Rafi.

"Not through the front door," Rafi answered positively. "I'd have heard someone come in."

"Not through the basement door either," Chaim added. "I locked it from the outside when I left. The only way to get in would be with a key, and the door didn't look forced."

"Any other ways to get into the house? The back door?" Tendall persisted.

"No." This time it was Elisheva who answered. "The back door is in the kitchen and I was in the kitchen having a snack until the lights went out. I would have seen someone come in or go out."

Again there was a brief silence.

"Could they have left from the basement door?" Tendall asked Chaim.

Chaim considered. "I locked it from the outside with a key," he repeated. "The twins don't have a key, so if they left through the basement, the door should be unlocked. I'll go check." He stood up.

"I'll go with you," Tendall said, also rising. "You can show me around your lab while we're at it."

This was precisely what Chaim had hoped to avoid, but he said nothing, merely indicating for the officer to come with him.

Chaim descended the stairs first, glancing quickly about the lab, but there was no sign of anything untoward. Tendall passed him and went to examine the door.

"It's still locked from the outside," Tendall said after a moment. "You're sure they had no key?"

"Yes, only my wife and I have keys to that door," Chaim said.

"Alright, show me what they did down here," Tendall asked, turning away from the door.

Chaim showed him the fused computer cables and gave a very simple and abbreviated description of his project. He wanted to keep the officer's attention on the missing twins, not on the MEC. His responsibility to his colleagues and sponsors weighed heavily on his conscience.

"Matter-energy conversion?" Tendall repeated, eyebrows raised. "Your machine can accomplish this?"

"There are still some bugs to work out," Chaim admitted, without elaborating. "It's not finished yet."

"And two ten-year-olds activated this unfinished machine and destroyed it and knocked the power off-line for the entire house." Tendall summed up his understanding of events.

"They didn't destroy the whole machine, just one computer," Chaim reiterated. "It's not as bad as it sounds. In the course of this project, I've accidentally destroyed a whole lot more than that."

He was anxious to make Tendall understand why he didn't think the twins would have run away. Yes, he was definitely annoyed that they had touched his equipment without permission, but he would just talk to them, explaining sternly that what they had done was wrong and explaining again why the lab was off-limits. It would all be okay. They hadn't done anything that couldn't be fixed.

"They didn't do anything that can't be fixed," he said out loud to Tendall.

"But maybe they didn't know that," Tendall pointed out.

Chaim shook his head, unconvinced.

"I know my kids," he insisted. "I just don't believe they ran away. Something else happened."

"Well, I'd be interested in hearing your explanation," Tendall returned. "As far as I can figure based on what the other kids have said, the only way they could have left the house would have been to climb out the second floor windows!"

With that, Tendall exited the lab, leaving Chaim gazing after him thoughtfully.

"Well, that didn't go so badly," Dena said optimistically. "Abba didn't really tell him any more than he told us about the project. Less, in fact."

She was still concerned about the privacy of Abba's machine.

"'Out the second floor window'?" Dovi repeated, laughing. "I never thought of trying that."

"And don't think of it now," Dena replied hastily, as the two of them returned to where the rest of the family was waiting.

Officer Tendall repeated his conclusions to Sarah. "If everyone is remembering accurately, then the twins must still be in the house. There is no sign they ever left. Are you sure you checked thoroughly?"

"Several times," Sarah insisted. "They must have got out the front door while the lights were out and Rafi didn't notice."

Rafi shook his head doubtfully but didn't contradict her. After all, what other explanation was there?

Tendall took note of the boy's expression but didn't comment on it. He reviewed his timeline of events one more time to make sure he had everything clear, then said, "I would like to take a look through the rest of the house real quick. Oh, and please provide a recent picture of both children," he requested.

"Of course," Sarah answered quickly. "Rafi can go through the house with you. Elisheva, please get a picture of Dovi and Dena from Cousin Avi's bar mitzvah. I think those are the most recent. Make sure they're clear ones."

Elisheva nodded her understanding and ran out of the room. Rafi got up to accompany Officer Tendall around the house. Chaim and Sarah were left facing each other.

"I can't believe we're dealing with something like this," Sarah mused out loud. "I'm so worried about them!"

Chaim leaned forward urgently, and said quietly, "Sarah, something else is going on inside the lab. Something strange, just before Officer Tendall came —"

"You're still thinking about your project?" Sarah interrupted incredulously. All she could think about now were the twins; nothing else seemed important.

"I think it's *related* to the twins being missing," Chaim said insistently. All the vague ideas that had been circling his brain all afternoon were coalescing together with the theory of the police officer that the twins must still be in the house. A rather incredible theory. "I didn't want to say this in front of Tendall just in case I'm wrong, but I'm starting to think that whatever the twins did was a lot more than simply overloading a few circuits."

Sarah was properly paying attention now. "What exactly is it you think they did?" she asked urgently. "Do you think they hurt themselves?" She stopped asking questions as Elisheva returned with the pictures.

"These are the clearest I could find," she said, looking curiously between the two of them. Sarah took the pictures from her.

"Thank you, sweetie, these are great," Sarah said, glancing at the photographs. Dovi's laughing green eyes and big grin looked back at her from one of them, Dena's more sedate expression from the other.

"You and Ahuva can go back to the playroom to play while we finish up here." She gently pushed Ahuva off her lap and both girls reluctantly went. She turned back to Chaim to resume their conversation, but before she could press him for further details, Tendall and Rafi returned from their tour of the house.

"Are those the pictures?" he asked Sarah, nodding at the pictures in her hand. She handed them over to him and he glanced at both photos, then tucked them into his jacket pocket together with his notepad.

"I'll have copies made of these down at the station," he informed them. "We'll distribute them and ask everyone to keep an eye out. As of now, I can't see any evidence of foul play. At least for a while, we're just going to have to wait and see how things play out." He looked at them all sympathetically. "I know this is hard, but hang in there. Chances are good they'll be back before night. If anything turns up please let us know, and I'll be in touch if we find out anything."

Chaim walked him to the door and shook his hand again. "Thank you for your help."

"My pleasure," Tendall replied, stepping out into the cold and snow.

Once he had gone, Chaim turned back to his family and said, "We davened and asked Hashem to help us find the twins. Now I need to do some *hishtadlus*. I think I should let Jeff know exactly what has been going on. With Hashem's help, we'll figure this out together."

11

JEFF ARRIVED AT THEIR HOME within twenty minutes. No one was happier to see him than the twins.

"Abba knows. He knows what happened to us,"
Dena asserted positively to her twin, her petite form
bouncing up and down excitedly. "He wouldn't have
called Dr. Schwartz otherwise."

"He didn't say that; you can't know for sure,"
Dovi was hesitant to get his hopes up. "All he told
Dr. Schwartz was that there was a problem in the
lab and he should come over as quickly as possible.
That's not the same as saying, 'The twins turned
themselves invisible and I need you help to put them
right.'"

He had such a comical and expressive way of

speaking that Dena couldn't help giggling a little.

"Well, maybe he doesn't know exactly what happened," she conceded, "but he knows we didn't run away or get kidnapped, or anything like that, I can tell. Why else would he have called in Dr. Schwartz instead of waiting for the police to find us? Together they'll figure out the details and how to fix us," she assured him confidently.

"Are you sure that it's possible to fix us?" Dovi asked anxiously, probably for the fiftieth time. "I'm still worried we're going to be stuck like this forever." He gestured to his insubstantial form.

Dena was getting tired of reassuring him, and of course, she didn't know for sure. All she could do was hope. And think. And listen. Oh yes, and interfere with the flow of electrical energy.

"Well, at least we can't say nothing interesting ever happens to us," Dovi observed dryly, when Dena failed to address his concerns. They were hovering around their father while he tested the outlet, plugging in various devices and seeing if they worked. Of course, they all did. He examined the radiator as well, but found nothing unusual. He returned to his computer and began typing. Dena watched intently over his shoulder.

"Should you be looking at that?" Dovi asked

her, using his stocky shoulders to block her view. "Maybe it's private."

"Well, it might be, but it concerns us," Dena returned, pushing him aside so she could see. "He's researching interactions between various forms of energy!" Dena cried exultantly. "See here, these symbols are one form of energy, these here are another." She pointed to the computer screen.

Dovi looked, but other than seeming vaguely familiar, the symbols on the screen meant nothing to him. "I'll take your word for it," he assured his sister. If Dena was happy, that was surely a good sign. But Dena was suddenly frowning.

"Wait, those aren't the right forms of energy!" she exclaimed, distressed. "Abba has the wrong symbols, I'm sure of it." She scrunched up her face, trying to control her disappointment.

Dovi was quick to comfort her. "I wouldn't worry," he consoled her. "If Abba is making a mistake he'll realize it eventually. And remember what happened the last time you underestimated Abba — we ended up like this. Just trust that Abba knows what he's doing."

Dena considered her brother's advice. He had a point, she had to admit. Abba was a smart man, and so was Dr. Schwartz. If anyone could solve this, they could. She just had to trust them and stop thinking she had to fix every problem herself. It wasn't easy; Dena did like to take care of things herself.

At that point Jeff arrived. He knocked on the lab door, and leaving his computer, Chaim got up and invited him in.

"So what's been going on here, Chaim?" Jeff asked without preamble. "I could tell when I spoke to you earlier that something was wrong. You sounded too distracted. The demonstration is scheduled for twelve o'clock tomorrow morning, so whatever the problem is, let's get working on it." He made a move toward the computers, the 'control room' of the lab, but Chaim put out a hand and stopped him.

"The problem isn't with the MEC, exactly," Chaim said slowly, wondering how to explain what he barely understood himself.

"Not with the MEC?" he repeated. "You mean it's working? How did you do it? And then what's the problem?" Jeff questioned curiously.

"The problem is with my kids, the twins, to be exact," Chaim began.

"The twins? What's the matter with them?" Jeff asked, concerned and confused. Why would Chaim want to discuss a problem with the twins with him? It wasn't like he had that much experience with children. "What's this all about, Chaim?" he asked again.

"I'll tell you, if you give me the chance," Chaim responded.

"Sorry," Jeff murmured, sitting down and waiting for Chaim to explain.

"I think the twins activated the MEC accidentally. And I think, actually I'm quite sure, they did it with the energy variable equation balanced."

Jeff's eyes opened wide as the implications of this went through his mind. "But didn't that have any impact on the MEC? Any time we tried that in simulations the whole machine fried!" He turned around to examine the MEC. "It looks fine to me," he added, puzzled but hopeful.

"It only destroyed one computer and a whole lot of wires and connecting cables. The MEC itself isn't damaged; I'm not sure why, but I checked it carefully. It's fine. And I already replaced the computer," Chaim assured him.

"Then this is good news," Jeff surmised, still puzzled. "I don't see the problem."

"The problem," Chaim repeated, "is that the twins are gone. Disappeared. No one has seen them for hours. The police were here just half an hour ago to get their information and start searching for them. I only figured out what they did by salvaging the hard drive from the old computer."

"That's why you sent me the equalized formula and asked me to run it again," Jeff exclaimed, as realization dawned. "Obviously the results in practice are somewhat different than the numbers and simulations indicate. It happens sometimes," he added philosophically. Then his face turned gravely serious. "What do you suppose happened to the twins?"

"I'm not a hundred percent sure, but I have a theory," Chaim confided. "A very strange theory and I'll need your help to prove or disprove it."

Jeff leaned forward, his eyes alight with interest. "Let's hear it."

Chaim told him about the second set of burned cables, about the strange, unexplained electrical discharges he had witnessed in two places at once, the outlet and the radiator, and Officer Tendall's determination that the twins couldn't have left through any of the house doors. Jeff listened intently, his blue eyes fixed on Chaim.

"My theory is that the twins never did leave, that they are, in fact, still here." Finally Chaim said it. He leaned back, waiting for Jeff's reaction.

But Jeff didn't understand. He looked searchingly around the lab, then back at Chaim. "Not much place in here to hide," he commented. "If they were in here we would see them."

Chaim held up his hand and said clearly, "Not if they were invisible."

Jeff gaped at him, unable to answer.

"Listen," Chaim said urgently, determined to explain. "The MEC is designed to convert matter to energy and then store that energy until it is converted back, right?"

"Right," Jeff, answered, agreeing. "But that's meant for things, Chaim, not people!" He could hardly grasp what Chaim was suggesting. It wasn't possible; it didn't make sense. There was absolutely no way the twins had been converted to energy— was there? That was just too far-fetched—wasn't it?

Suddenly, Jeff didn't quite know what to think anymore. His scientific, logical mind argued with his warm and compassionate heart. What would happen to a human being who was converted to energy? Could he survive? Jeff had spent so much time with Chaim's family, he felt like Chaim's kids were as good as his own. He couldn't bear to think of anything happening to the twins.

Why, they had all just been together at the Shabbos meal this past Friday night. In his mind's eye, he could see Dovi's mischievous look as he pulled some prank, and how Dena helped her mother serve each course, just like a little lady. The two younger girls had peppered him with a multitude of questions about every subject imaginable and he had happily tried to come up with answers for them. He and Rafi had had their usual Friday night study hour after the meal. Rafi was teaching him the laws of Shabbos. Rafi taught in such a sensitive and mature way that Jeff was never embarrassed that he knew so much less than a young teenager.

"What would happen to a person turned into energy?" he whispered to Chaim hoarsely.

Chaim had watched the changes of expression pass over his friend's face and Jeff's question now confirmed that Jeff had accepted the possibility of his theory. He was satisfied with that; with Jeff's help he was sure everything would be all right. He felt a profound sense of relief.

The twins shared his feelings.

"He did understand; I told you," Dena whispered, her eyes shining proudly.

"Yeah, he did, and he must think there's something he can do about it or he wouldn't be so calm," Dovi added, his natural optimism rising to the fore again.

"He also has Dr. Schwartz to help him figure it

out," Dena added. "Between the two of them I bet there's nothing they can't do."

Dovi wasn't sure he would go that far, but he understood the sentiment. He too had a lot of confidence in his father and Dr. Schwartz. Both were brilliant men.

"Should we help them along again?" he asked Dena. "You know, blow things up or something?"

She glanced at him, a funny expression on her face. "Hey," he defended himself, correctly interpreting her look, "ordinarily right now I'd be out in the snow, building an igloo or something. I'm bored. I need something to do."

Dena glanced at the clock. Her own watch had stopped working at the moment she had activated the MEC and still showed 11:52, but the clock on the wall showed 4:30. They had only been like this for four and a half hours? It felt like longer; her sense of time passing was still warped. But she sympathized with Dovi's predicament. The truth was she was bored too. The only thing she had really been able to do was cause the sparks that alerted their father to their presence. Inactivity didn't sit well with either of them.

"Interacting with the energy flow already had the effect we wanted it to," Dena demurred. "I'm not sure we really need to do it again."

114

The sensation had been quite uncomfortable, but it had been necessary and it served its purpose. She couldn't see any reason to repeat the experience. Even if they were bored.

After a few moments thought, Chaim responded to Jeff's question. "I can't be entirely sure, but I think in some ways they're still themselves. The only thing I can figure is that they were trying to communicate with me the only way they could think of. They seemed to be making a concerted effort; it couldn't have been random."

Jeff let out a sigh of relief. "Well, if that's true, at least they're alive. But that's not how the machine is supposed to work; you know that. It's supposed to store the energy, not leave it free floating around the environment!

"Hey!" he said in a flash of understanding. "That's why the MEC wasn't destroyed."

Chaim waited curiously for his friend to explain.

"The MEC was always destroyed, in simulations and experiments, because it couldn't handle the amount of energy it was being asked to store. But it isn't storing the twins so it wasn't destroyed. But why isn't it storing the twins, if that's how the machine was designed to work?" Jeff repeated his previous question.

"I don't know quite how to explain that," Chaim admitted. "Clearly the MEC functions differently in practice than in the simulations. Maybe it has something to do with them being human. Every time we tested the machine, and in all the simulations, the subject was always simple matter, without its own energy source."

Jeff pondered that. "Could be," he agreed.

"Hey, Chaim," he added, after a pause. "Remember, there was one material that sort of worked once, like a year ago. Maybe we can get ahold of that."

Chaim knew immediately what he was referring to. "You mean that substance that Ira Evans came up with in the lab at Mark Technologies? Come on, Jeff, that stuff was completely unstable. It was practically a bomb waiting to explode in our faces. That's why we fired Ira, remember? He didn't tell us about the instabilities and there was that accident. We're lucky no one was killed!"

"Okay, okay," Jeff raised his hands in surrender. He had known that suggestion was a long shot. "But what do we do now?"

"Now," Chaim replied, glad to finally get back to the point, "we figure out how to get the twins back."

◆◆◆ ◆ ◆◆◆

"Elisheva," Sarah called, "please set the table for dinner. Ahuva'le, come, we're going to straighten up the playroom together."

The twins might be missing, but the other children and the house still needed to be cared for. She went through the motions, but her mind whirled as she mentally reviewed the theory her husband had shared with her before Jeff had come. The twins turned to energy? She wasn't completely sure she wouldn't rather they be out somewhere in the darkening winter afternoon, than wandering about the house as invisible beings.

"It's Dena's job to set the table," Elisheva protested, without looking up from the project she was making.

"Well, she can't right now, can she?" Sarah pointed out. "So you're going to have to do it for her. And be sure to set a place for Dr. Schwartz."

Elisheva jumped up gleefully. "Is Dr. Schwartz going to eat dinner with us on a weeknight?" she asked surprised.

"He's working with your Abba. You wouldn't expect him to go hungry, would you?"

"Of course not," Elisheva answered, and bounced away to the kitchen.

They hadn't shared Chaim's theory with the children, figuring it was too complicated to explain to them. Sarah suggested telling Rafi of Chaim's suspicions, and Chaim said he'd think about it. Sarah hoped he'd agree; she had a feeling Rafi could use a show of confidence right now.

Sarah watched her daughter leave.

How can she be so cheerful when things are so wrong here? Sarah wondered.

But that wasn't fair, she knew. Elisheva was only seven, incapable of understanding what the twins' absence meant. To her the twins were simply gone for the afternoon and any moment now the door would open and they would come trooping back in, full of stories of their various activities. She half expected it herself, though if Chaim was right, that wasn't a possibility.

Energy?! she asked herself again. *How could something like that possibly happen?*

"Ima!" Ahuva was tugging at her sleeve. "Are you listening to me?" The little girl stood in front of her with her chubby hands on her hips.

"Sorry, sweetie, what did you say?" Sarah tried to focus her attention.

"We're supposed to be cleaning up, remember? But you're just sitting there staring. What are you thinking about?" Ahuva was perceptive enough to know her mother was distracted and distressed, but too young to understand the cause.

"You're right," Sarah forced a little laugh. "I was just thinking about the twins and I forgot what we were supposed to be doing. Thanks for reminding me. How about if you do the dolls and I'll do the blocks, okay?"

Ahuva nodded her head in assent, her curls waving back and forth, and Sarah returned to her thoughts, her hands going through the motions of cleaning up while her mind wandered. Rafi came into the playroom where his mother and sister were finishing up.

"Abba's not going to be able to study math with me tonight, is he?" Rafi asked abruptly, after watching them for a few minutes.

"Oh, honey, I'm sorry, but I really doubt it," Sarah answered. "Even without this whole mess with the twins, Abba has to be ready for that demonstration tomorrow. Is there anything I can help you with?" she offered.

Rafi shook his head, unsurprised. "No, thanks," he declined. "Actually, Dena already showed me some tricks this morning. I guess that'll have to be enough." He paused. "Are you sure there's going to be school tomorrow?" He couldn't imagine going to school with the twins missing, going about his day like normal. How would he even concentrate on his tests?

As though reading his thoughts, Sarah said softly, "I think there will be school. We can only hope they're back before then." She patted his cheek and left the room.

12

RAFI ABSENTLY PUSHED HIS LASAGNA around his plate with his fork as he listened to his father's and Dr. Schwartz's intent conversation. They, too, hardly paid attention to their food as they debated abstract concepts that Rafi could scarcely comprehend. In fact, he only understood about one out of every five words and lost the thread of the conversation fairly quickly.

Still, he listened. The table felt strangely quiet and subdued without the twins. At the other end of the table, his mother was trying to coax Ahuva into eating her food.

"I can't eat it, it hurts my throat," Ahuva whined, pushing away the plate in front of her.

Both Ahuva and Elisheva picked up on the strained mood at the table. Elisheva responded to it by becoming quiet and thoughtful, but Ahuva became clingy and kvetchy. The fact that she still wasn't feeling well didn't help.

"You need to eat, sweetie," Sarah told her, also trying to listen to the men's conversation with half an ear. "Otherwise you'll be so hungry."

But Ahuva stubbornly closed her mouth and turned her face away, her little red lips shut tightly. Sarah sighed and gave up. Ordinarily she might have insisted that Ahuva eat the food she had prepared for her, but tonight she didn't have the strength for an argument. Her youngest child could be very stubborn.

"Alright, you can have some yogurt. That will feel good on your throat." Sarah felt this was a reasonable compromise.

Fortunately, Ahuva found this suggestion acceptable and Sarah watched with relief as she went to bring the yogurt from the refrigerator. She glanced at Rafi's full plate, then caught his eye.

"You need to eat, too," she told him gently.

Rafi swallowed hard. "It's dark outside," he said, nodding his dark head toward the kitchen window. Ima turned to look. Blackness had fallen, concealing the snow-covered yard. Through the window she could see the half moon, providing just enough illumination for the bare tree branches to cast shadows upon the snow. Night had fallen and the twins were nowhere to be seen.

With a start, she remembered that Rafi had not heard Abba's theory about the twins' extraordinary transformation. He was surely still picturing the twins wandering alone in the cold and dark and snow, maybe lost or hurt. *That isn't fair to him*, Sarah thought. *We have to tell him what we suspect.* She tuned in again to what Chaim was saying.

"… the electrons to move beyond a certain speed threshold —" He was gesturing with his hands while he spoke and Jeff was nodding in agreement.

"Abba," she interrupted gently, "I think it's time to tell Rafi about the theory you're working on." She nodded significantly at their older son.

Chaim caught her look and regarded his son. Rafi looked at him hopefully, lowering his fork with the food uneaten. Chaim felt a sudden rush of compassion for the boy. Sarah had always maintained that Rafi had an unspoken disappointment that Dena had so much more in common with their father than he did, but Chaim had never been able to see it. He felt a pang of guilt. Maybe he had gotten so involved in his project that he neglected to let Rafi know how proud he was of his mature, responsible oldest child.

Rafi was still looking at him now with a mixture of expectancy and confusion, wanting his father to confide in him, but afraid he wouldn't understand what his father was talking about. At the same time, he couldn't figure out why everyone was still focused on Abba's project when the twins were unaccounted for.

Sarah drew the attention of both little girls as Chaim started from the beginning, with a brief description of the MEC, similar to what Dena had said just that morning, and then explaining what he thought must have happened when the twins were in the lab. Rafi listened, his mouth falling open as Abba finished speaking. He looked back and forth between his father and Dr. Schwartz, waiting for someone to say that this was just a joke. But no one spoke. The silence grew until, unexpectedly, Elisheva spoke up.

"But if the twins turned into energy, where is their *neshamah*?"

Her question was met with more blank silence. Finally, Sarah answered, "I'm sure it's all fine, sweetheart. Hashem can take care of it, don't worry."

Then, trying to distract her, she asked, "Can you please start clearing the table?"

Rafi finally found his voice. "Can a person survive that?" he whispered.

"We think so," his father said reassuringly. "In fact we think the twins have already tried to communicate with me."

He didn't elaborate on how, despite the questioning look in Rafi's eyes. He also hadn't meant for the girls to overhear, but obviously Elisheva had, and had at least partially understood what he had said.

She didn't at all appear to have been paying attention, he mused. *I'll have to be careful what I say around her in the future.*

"So how will we change them back?" Rafi wanted to know, getting to the heart of the matter. "We can't leave them like that forever!"

Chaim and Jeff exchanged glances. "That's what we're trying to figure out now," Jeff answered. "We have a long night ahead of us, but we won't stop until they're safely back to normal."

With a sudden burst of inspiration, Chaim offered, "Maybe there's some way you can help us, Rafi."

Rafi's eyes lit up. "Can I?" he asked hopefully. "How?"

Sarah interjected before Chaim could respond. "You have exams tomorrow don't you? You need to finish studying and get a good night's sleep."

Rafi turned to her. "Oh, Ima, I finished studying, and this is really important. Please let me work with Abba?" he pleaded.

Sarah didn't answer for a few moments. She recognized that Rafi felt somewhat responsible for what had happened to the twins, and maybe it would do his conscience good to be a part of the rescue effort. On the other hand, she felt like this was a matter for the adults to deal with, and he shouldn't have to be bothered with it.

"I'm not a baby," Rafi added, as though reading her thoughts. "Abba thinks I can help."

"Okay," his mother relented, sighing. "You can help."

Immediately, Elisheva piped up, "I want to help too."

"You're too young," Rafi said the familiar refrain.

"If you can help, I can too!" Elisheva shot back.

"I'm thirteen; you're seven. There's a big difference," Rafi argued.

"I want to stay up late and help in Abba's lab," Elisheva appealed again to her parents.

Here, Sarah put her foot down.

"Not a chance," she informed her daughter. "You and Ahuva are going to take baths and get ready for bed, with no complaining."

Her tone brooked no argument and for once Elisheva and Ahuva meekly left the table and ran upstairs. Ima began to load the dishwasher, saying to Rafi, "You can help Abba once you're completely ready for school tomorrow."

Rafi nodded his understanding, and he too left the table.

Once he was out of earshot, Sarah turned to Chaim and asked quietly, "What is it exactly you think he can do?"

"I can find something. I think the important thing right now is for him to feel useful. And he may actually be able to contribute; you never know. Right now, we're under a deadline. We don't know how long the twins can maintain their molecular cohesion while in this state. We need to use all the heads we can get."

Sarah closed the dishwasher door with a snap, her face resolute. "Then I'm going to help too," she stated with an air of finality.

The twins had been quietly watching everyone else eat. Every few minutes Dovi moaned about how hungry he was. He had already missed lunch and was now missing dinner too, but being hungry herself and unable to help him, Dena said nothing. At Abba's words, however, the two exchanged glances. Dena's was one of horror, and Dovi's was one of puzzlement.

"What does that mean?" Dovi demanded to know. "What does that mean, 'maintain molecular cohesion'?" He could tell from Abba's tone and the worried expressions on Ima's and Dr. Schwartz's faces that it was something serious.

"I think it means that Abba's worried about our atoms staying together. He thinks we're going to … I don't know, disintegrate or something." Dena told him, her brow furrowed as she tried to understand exactly what her father was saying.

"What?!" Dovi exclaimed. "How come you didn't say anything about this?"

"Because," Dena answered with some asperity, "I didn't know about it. I don't know why Abba thinks it will happen. Maybe he's just guessing, or maybe he knows something I don't. Not maybe, for sure," she amended quickly.

The four of them will come up with something, she reassured herself. *They have to. We're running out of time. Even if we don't lose molecular cohesion, we're go-*

ing to starve if we can't eat soon. Or at least Dovi will.

"So how does this molecular cohesion work?" Dovi asked, trying to distract himself, both from his fears and from his hunger.

"Molecular cohesion is when particles, you know, pieces of matter, hold together to form something," Dena tried to explain. "Losing molecular cohesion means the molecules start to separate and go away from each other. I wonder why Abba thinks that will happen to us."

"Is there anything we can do to prevent this from happening?" Dovi pressed her.

"Not that I can think of, but really, I wouldn't know," Dena replied, once again feeling the pressure to always know the right answer. But she was only ten; there wasn't enough time for her to learn everything yet, and this was way outside anything she had studied. Whatever she did know came from a few paragraphs she had read in a biology book she found once in the school library.

Dovi recognized the tension rising in her by the way her face flushed and her hands clenched and he quickly backed off.

"It's okay," he assured her. "Abba would know and if not he'll find out. We just need to listen carefully in case they say something we need to do."

Dena agreed with this. They would have to be careful not to miss anything.

Ima was busy putting Elisheva and Ahuva to sleep. Rafi was preparing his lunch for tomorrow. But Abba and Dr. Schwartz had their heads bent over an open folder on the kitchen table, speaking quietly but intently. They seemed to be arguing about something, and Dena leaned in close, trying to follow the points each one was making.

This isn't going so well, she admitted to herself after listening for a while. Ordinarily, when her father spoke to her about science or math his words resonated with her and she clearly understood what he told her. But the science talk between the two men was like listening to some foreign language. Vaguely recognizable, but almost totally incomprehensible.

Why can't I understand what they're saying? she wondered. *Is it being caused by this loss of molecular cohesion Abba talked about? Or do I just really know a lot less than I thought?*

If she was honest with herself, she suspected it was the latter. Abba must water down whatever he told her enough so she could understand it. She had always thought she did such a good job of not being proud over her intellectual capabilities, but now she realized that pride really had got the best of her. She understood everything Abba said to her because he made sure she would. Just like she did when she explained things to others.

A watered down version of a watered down version, she thought, somewhat amused. She wasn't discouraged for longer than a moment to realize how far she still had to go to reach her goal of being a great scientist. If anything, she felt a renewed surge of determination that one day she would be fluent in that fascinating foreign language.

Dovi was watching her expectantly, waiting for her to explain what it was they needed to do. Noting the blank expression on her face, he prodded anxiously. "What are they saying? Have they figured anything out? Are we dying?"

Dena wanted to answer his questions as she had always done, to reassure him, to return the spark of mischief and fun to his eyes. But she couldn't.

"Dovi, I'm sorry, but I can't follow what they're saying," she confessed, a little embarrassed by this admission. "We're going to have to trust that if there's something we need to do they'll find a way to let us know." She broke off as Dovi slapped an exasperated hand against his forehead.

"This is just getting worse and worse," he

lamented. He strode over to the table, to the chair Rafi had recently vacated.

Dena watched as though in slow motion as Dovi thoughtlessly let himself drop onto the chair.

"No, Dovi, stop!" she cried out, but it was too late. She watched helplessly as Dovi crashed through the chair, his arms pin-wheeling wildly, and kept going, straight through the floor and out of sight.

"Dovi!" Dena cried again. She raced out of the kitchen to the basement stairs, but skidded to a halt when she got there.

The lab door had been shut! How was she going to get down? She couldn't turn the door handle. She had been going up and down all day, but she realized now someone had always opened the door for her.

Dena stood indecisively in front of the door, terribly worried about Dovi, not sure how to get to him to help him. *Could he be hurt? How long would he keep falling?* The not knowing, and not being able to ask, or to run to a reference book and check it up, was beginning to eat at her.

You could go through the door, a small voice whispered in her mind. But she shied away from that thought. Walk through a door? No way, she just couldn't. What if she got stuck?

Be sensible, the voice persisted. *How would you get stuck? You've been passing your hands through things all afternoon without any problem.*

But this is bigger, she answered the voice. *This is different. What if it messes up my own molecular structure in some way?*

You're rationalizing your fears, the voice argued relentlessly. *Do this for Dovi; do this for him because he would do it for you.*

That decided it. Dena took a deep breath and, without giving herself any more time for fear or doubt, she passed through the basement door and found herself on the other side, at the top of the stairs.

Well, that wasn't so bad.

Letting out her breath in a sudden release of tension, Dena called down the stairs, "Dovi! Are you down there? Are you okay?"

To her immense relief she heard an answer.

"I'm here." He sounded dazed but otherwise all right.

Dena quickly descended the stairs and stopped when she caught sight of her brother. His downward progress had been halted ... by the MEC computer!

Blue and silver sparks were shooting up around her brother and for the third time, the oppressive odor of melted rubber surrounded them.

Dovi was lying on the computer table, half his body invisible to her as they slid into the objects around him. But the part of him she did see appeared distinctly worse for wear. His sandy colored hair was standing on end, his face had black soot marks, and his light blue button-down shirt and dark blue pants were singed and blackened in various places.

"Are you alright?" she asked nervously, as she put out a hand and helped him off the table.

He groaned as he stood upright, and then he tried to brush himself off. It did little good. He remained as disheveled as before.

"What are the chances," he demanded with all the dignity he could muster, "that I would fall through the floor and land on Abba's machine, breaking it again?"

"It's a good thing you did land on it," Dena told him after ascertaining that he wasn't really hurt. "Who knows how long you'd have kept falling otherwise?"

A thought occurred to Dovi. "Why aren't we falling through the floor now? How is it holding us up?"

A similar question had crossed Dena's mind, but she just shrugged, having no answer.

"I guess we should just be glad it is," Dovi said after a moment.

They both stood there quietly, lost in their own thoughts. Finally, Dena looked up at her brother.

"What do we do now?" she wanted to know.

Dovi straightened in surprise. Until now, he had been the one asking questions, and Dena had been the one providing answers. But it seemed her answers had run out. Dovi was a natural leader, unused to taking the backseat, but he had been really out of his league. Now, however, Dena was asking his opinion; it was time to take charge.

"Now," he replied with more confidence than he felt, "we draw Abba and Dr. Schwartz back down here. This is where they could do us the most good."

"And how do we get them to come down?" Dena questioned. "Last I saw they looked perfectly happy to continue their conference at the kitchen table and scribble equations on napkins."

Dovi tried to consider his options. He had to admit, they were limited. Usually, when it came time to solving a problem, he could talk his way out of it or something. But now, he could yell until he lost his voice and no one would hear him; no one except one person who was as helpless as he was. Dovi slapped his hand against his thigh in frustration. He was hungry, he was tired, he was dirty, and he was definitely finding it hard to think.

Dena watched him patiently. She understood exactly how he felt. She felt just as helpless, hungry, and harassed. She didn't blame him for not knowing what to do.

"Well, they'll come down on their own eventually," Dovi finally muttered, half to himself. "They'll see this mess and know we've been here, that we're still here, that we haven't lost molecular cohesion or whatever."

Dena hid a small smile. Her brother might put on a show of being a clown sometimes, but she had long suspected he caught more than he let on. He liked to have a good time, but every once in a while, those who knew him best got a glimpse of a sharp and active mind. And no one knew him better than she did.

"But we'll go back up and try to keep listening to them. All we can do right now is keep track of their progress," Dovi added.

"Uh, Dovi?" Dena felt she had better mention the fact that the basement door was closed. She was sure he would get frustrated about this all over again, but he surprised her.

"I just fell through the ceiling," he shrugged. "How hard can it be to walk through a door? Besides, you've already done it and came out alright." He eyed her critically, as though to make sure she really was in one piece. Apparently satisfied, he made his way to the stairs, Dena trailing him. Somehow walking through the door again didn't seem as scary with Dovi alongside her.

The dynamics upstairs had changed slightly since Dovi's tumble through the floor. Sarah was upstairs supervising the girls' baths. Rafi had completed his preparations for school the next morning and had pulled up a chair next to Chaim and was leaning over the table, paying careful attention to every word spoken.

Chaim and Jeff were also leaning toward each other, their voices raised in heated debate. Every few seconds, one man cut across the other's words impatiently. Dena and Dovi stared in surprise. Their father and Jeff had been the best of friends for as long as the twins could remember. But the tense situation was clearly raising some strong emotions. Behind his glasses, Rafi's wide brown eyes went back and forth between the two scientists, trying to keep up with the argument.

Suddenly the sound of a throat clearing cut

across the arguing. Both men turned to find Sarah standing in the doorway, her hands on her hips.

"This isn't helping," she pointed out quietly. "We have a time limit, and arguing is wasting the precious time we do have." She too pulled up a chair and perched on the edge of it, straightening her flowered *tichel* as she settled herself. "In a minute I have to go back up and read to the girls and get them into bed, but before that, we are going to decide on a plan of action." She looked between the three of them, making sure she had their attention. "So let's prioritize. What's first?"

Chaim glanced at Jeff, who nodded to him. "First we need to be able to locate the twins. There should be two large concentrations of energy marking their locations. We need a way to detect them."

"That's where we disagree," Jeff put in, wagging a thick finger. "Right now, we can't come up with a way to find them. I think we should run some tests on the MEC, make sure it's up and running, until we think of something."

There was a moment of thoughtful silence. It was Rafi who finally broke it.

"Abba, you said the outlet and radiator were sparking at the same time, right? So you knew where they were at that moment. That's how you figured out what happened to them. It had to be on purpose, they were trying to communicate with you. So they can do it again. All we have to do is be on the lookout for strange power surges," Rafi finished nervously. He so badly wanted to help. He held his breath, waiting to see what his father thought of his suggestion.

His father smiled at him. "You have a good point there, son," he acknowledged. "Maybe we should leave it to the twins to let us know where they are. They did it before; hopefully they can do it again." He smiled kindly at Rafi, who felt his nervousness drain away to be replaced with a feeling of warmth and pride.

"Great," Sarah said briskly. "So then what?"

There was a thoughtful pause. "Then we figure out how to reverse the process." Jeff offered.

"Any idea how?" Sarah persisted.

After another silence, Chaim said, "It's possible that if the machine is activated again with the proper setting and directed at the twins' location, the energy will be retransformed into matter."

He didn't sound terribly sure and Jeff was shaking his head pessimistically. Even Rafi could tell that it took a giant leap of faith to come to a conclusion like that. Wishful thinking, more like. Dena and Dovi exchanged nervous glances.

From upstairs came the sound of the girls calling Ima to come read to them, but for the moment she ignored it. Rafi sat very still, and the men carefully did not look at each other.

"Why do I get a bad feeling about this?" Sarah finally asked, very quietly.

"Because retransforming the twins has its dangers," Jeff admitted. "Probably more dangers than I'm aware of."

He didn't elaborate on what those dangers were. Dena wished he would. She felt like she could accept the whole thing better if she had a full understanding of what to expect, if she knew exactly what was going to happen. Dovi, by contrast, was happy that every little detail of the dangers that awaited them wasn't being spelled out.

What I don't know, I can't worry about, he told himself, *and besides, it looks like Dena is worried enough for both of us. But that's just business as usual.*

Sarah stared hard at her husband and his partner, her green eyes intense. For a moment it seemed as though she might ask about the dangers mentioned, but then she apparently decided against it. She stood, and with folded arms, announced that she was returning to Elisheva and Ahuva, who were calling her with increasing volume, but that when she returned they would get to work circumventing these possible dangers. Then she left the kitchen and headed upstairs.

Two freshly bathed girls greeted her. Sarah breathed in the scent of soap and shampoo, her children's scent. She took a moment to cuddle them close, not wanting to ever let go.

But she had to.

All she wanted to do was protect her children, always, from all harm, but that was just not possible. She knew this, but she also knew that it was her job to watch over them to the best of her abilities.

Sarah felt like she had failed her twins today. That fact left her mind reeling, her emotions raw. Holding onto the little girls wouldn't help the twins, she knew, but she couldn't help it. She couldn't let her security fail again.

Elisheva's hair was a tangled mass of wet curls, framing her face and spilling about her shoulders. Gently, Sarah straightened her unruly locks and sent her to brush her teeth. Ahuva seemed to be feeling somewhat better, though her voice was still hoarse and her eyes still a little too bright. Sarah gave Ahuva her medicine, noting with relief that Ahuva no longer protested taking it.

"It's not really so yucky," she informed her

mother solemnly. "It tastes kind of like cherries."

"Ima," Elisheva peered at her mother from under her blanket. "If Dena stays energy forever, can I have the top bunk?"

Sarah felt a jolt go through her stomach at Elisheva's words. *She doesn't understand what she's saying,* she reminded herself before answering.

"Dena is coming back, so you just stay right where you are," Sarah stated positively, allowing no room for doubt.

Sarah said Shema with them and then tucked both girls into their respective beds. As she kissed her goodnight, Ahuva grabbed her hand.

"Ima, are you sad today?" she asked, her other hand tucked under her round chin.

Sarah took one of the warm little hands in her own. "A little, sweetie," she replied, honestly.

"Why?" Ahuva asked innocently.

"Because Dena and Dovi are not here, and I miss them, and I'm very worried about them," Sarah explained, trying to keep it simple. She certainly didn't want to scare Ahuva right as she was going to sleep. Ahuva was already prone to nightmares, often waking up in the middle of the night, crying and frightened, needing to be reassured that everything was all right, that her parents were there.

Their pediatrician assured them that it was a passing phase, but in the meantime, they tried to keep her pre-bedtime thoughts happy and peaceful.

But as for herself, Sarah's stomach was knotting up with fear and worry, and it was only with great effort that she maintained her calm façade in front of the girls.

"We have to trust in Hashem to bring Dena and Dovi back to us safely," Sarah added, as much to herself as to her daughter. *I can hardly explain what's going on to myself, much less to a four-year-old.*

"I'll daven to Hashem to bring them back," Ahuva said seriously.

Sarah smiled in spite of her worries. "That would be wonderful, darling. I hope Hashem listens to you. You know, Hashem especially loves the *tefillos* of little children," she added, and then a thought struck her. "Would you like me to help you say some Tehillim?"

"I want to also," Elisheva put in immediately.

So, with the girls on either side of her, Sarah read from the Tehillim for some time, while they repeated her words. When she noticed Elisheva yawning and Ahuva's eyes drooping, she stood up and resettled the girls into bed. She kissed both girls one more time, and left the room, leaving the door partially open behind her.

JEFF SHOVED AN OPEN NOTEBOOK in Rafi's direction. The page was covered in math equations, symbols, formulas, Rafi wasn't even sure what. Jeff was sitting in front of the computer, typing at a rapid clip, examining the screen, and then clearing it with an impatient shake of his head. Rafi was reading out the numbers to him, one line at a time. He felt like they had been at this for hours and his head was beginning to ache.

Chaim was replacing the wires attached to the MEC for the third time that day, and again replacing the computer hard drive. While he worked he muttered to himself.

"I can't believe I'm doing this again. I'll never

get any real work done at this rate. Why on earth would they have ruined this another time?"

No one answered him. They were all tired and worried, and they didn't know any more than he did.

None of them looked up at the sound of footsteps on the stairs, but then Sarah came into view carrying a large tray. The rich smell of coffee filled the air, mixing with the mouthwatering scent of freshly baked cookies.

"A little refreshments," Sarah commented, putting the tray down on a table. "Looks like everyone could use some."

She handed her husband a large glass coffee mug. Wisps of steam rose gently from the dark brew as Chaim gratefully wrapped his hands around the hot cup.

"For you," Sarah continued, handing an identical cup to Jeff. He too accepted it with a murmured word of thanks. "And Rafi, some hot cocoa," she gave him his mug, leaving the last cup on the tray for herself. Then she passed around a plate, inviting them each to help themselves. "Oatmeal-chocolate-chip," she told them as they bit in. "Now, where were we?"

The brief interlude had done its job. They each returned to their tasks, refreshed and alert. Chaim had finished repairing the MEC, and was now working with Sarah, modifying some instruments.

"What exactly are we doing with these?" Sarah asked as they worked. Chaim had not really explained and she found herself wanting to fill the heavy silence that lay between them.

Chaim connected the two devices with an adapter plug before answering. "I'm modifying these two machines into a kinetic energy sensor. I'm hoping that if this works, we'll be able to identify the twins' exact location."

Sarah thought about that as she held each machine in place while her husband modified them to perform a function other than the ones they had been built to perform. Each piece was about the size of her hand, metallic, with a screen on one side showing glowing red numbers, and another screen on the other side with blinking green numbers. On the edges were buttons of various sizes.

She wasn't sure how she was functioning. A blinding panic threatened to overcome her whenever she allowed her mind to dwell on what they were going to attempt. She only knew she had to help in any way she could, whether by becoming an overnight assistant lab technician or by davening for her children's safety as only a mother could daven. Or both at the same time.

"Hand me that screwdriver, please," Chaim requested, looking up briefly from the cable he had just inserted into both machines.

Sarah handed him the tool and watched him remove the back of one of the machines, revealing coils of different colored wires inside.

"You take the white and red wires," Chaim instructed her. "I'll take the blue and yellow. When I tell you, remove your wires and place them in each other's holes. Then I'll do the same."

Sarah indicated that she understood his instructions, then waited for him to give her the word. Chaim tweaked something she couldn't see, and then opened his mouth to speak, but before he could say anything, the peal of the doorbell chimed throughout the house.

The four of them looked at each other. Who could be ringing their doorbell at ten o'clock at night?

Dovi tried to sniff the leftover cookies on the plate as his mother went to see who was at the door. Although he couldn't actually smell anything, his mouth started watering as he imagined the rich smell of melting chocolate, and the sweet, chewy taste of the cookies. He gave a moan of longing.

Dena was curled up on the floor, her head resting on her arm, her eyes open, but glazed with fatigue. The time was somewhat later than their usual bedtime, and it had been a very long, tiring day. Even hunger couldn't get her back on her feet. All she wanted to do was sleep.

How ironic that someone made of energy is so low on it, she thought with an inward chuckle. She thought of her bed, her soft, warm comforter; how much better that would be than the floor. Not that she could actually feel the floor. If she concentrated, she could stick her hand straight through it. She still wasn't sure why they didn't just fall and keep falling — she was just glad that they weren't. Things were complicated enough.

Her mother returned to the basement followed by another figure. Dena squinted to make out who it was, and sat up with a start of surprise as she recognized Officer Tendall. Dovi too turned sharply away from the cookie tray to regard the police officer curiously.

Chaim rose to his feet and pushed up his glasses with one finger. "Officer Tendall!" he exclaimed in a surprised voice.

Tendall surveyed the scene in the lab with interest. "I stopped by to see if there were any developments," he explained in that mild tone of his. "But it looks like you all are involved in some sort of project." He raised his eyebrows inquiringly.

Chaim and Sarah and Jeff exchanged glances. Suddenly not tired anymore, Dena got up and went to stand next to her twin. Rafi looked from one adult to another, wondering how they would explain. Jeff had his gaze on Chaim, a cautious look on his face.

"Chaim," he began, rising from his chair, but broke off as Chaim shook his head to forestall him. Jeff threw up his hands in resignation and sat back down.

"Officer, the project we're involved with is finding the twins," Chaim stated flatly.

Tendall raised his eyebrows as he leaned back against a table and crossed his arms over his chest. "I'm listening."

And so once again Chaim launched into the tale of how he developed the MEC, was called out of the house, and the twins made their way into the lab. He recounted the unusual events with the electricity, and the officer's own observations that led him to the conclusion that the twins were still in the house, just in an altered form.

Tendall listened, his expression never changing. When Chaim finished speaking, Tendall addressed Jeff.

"And you agree with his analysis of the situation? I mean, it is a little hard to swallow."

Jeff didn't look happy. Secrecy was always so important; they were always on guard not to let anything slip about the crucial aspects of their experiments and inventions, always aware that someone might hear about their work and claim it as his own. It was hard for him to understand how Chaim could now just reveal the deepest secrets of the project to a total stranger.

For a moment Jeff wavered, unsure how to respond to the officer's question. Then he caught Chaim's eye. Jeff had known Chaim for a long time and trusted him implicitly. Shouldn't he trust him now, too? And these were Chaim's kids at risk here. What was all the secrecy worth when compared to the lives of those two ten-year-olds? And Tendall had an air about him that made you want to trust him.

"I believe that Dr. Abrams' view of the situation is accurate," he finally answered. "We're working on how to retrieve them. We're afraid we may have a time limit." He explained their theory that the twins might not to be able to maintain energy form indefinitely.

Tendall seemed to be considering the information they had just presented to him. They all waited tensely for his reaction.

"You realize that the police have been searching

for those children, with increasing concern I might add, all evening. When were you going to have us call off our efforts?" He stared at them all sternly. "I need to let the station know right away."

He reached for his radio, but his hand stopped midway as Jeff called, "Wait!" Tendall raised his eyebrows at him questioningly. "You're right, we completely forgot about notifying you," Jeff agreed hastily, feeling he had this one chance to get through to the officer and maybe salvage their project. "But you can't just tell the whole police force what we're doing here. This has to stay secret!"

Tendall shook his head. "The police are busy searching for kids who you say aren't out there while they should be helping people affected by the snow-storm. I have a responsibility to report this."

"Of course you should call off the search," Chaim said in an appeasing tone. "But isn't there some way you could do it without giving all the details of what is going on over here? Honestly, at this point I think it would do more harm than good, especially for the children."

Officer Tendall looked at him questioningly. What did telling the police force about the MEC have to do with rescuing the twins?

Chaim hurried to explain. "If you report this,

the media will get ahold of it and we'll be bombarded with requests for interviews, demonstrations, who knows what else, not to mention the reaction from our company board members, child welfare, anyone who can get in our way. We need to keep this quiet until the twins are safe."

Tendall had to acknowledge that Chaim had a point. The safety of the twins must be of paramount importance. He nodded his head slowly and Chaim, Sarah, and Jeff all exhaled with relief as he lowered his hand away from his radio. Chaim felt his opinion of Officer Tendall rise several notches.

"I'll radio the station that the missing twins are back home, and I'm following up on the case, which they are, and I am. And then," he said, symbolically rolling up his sleeves, "I want to help."

"Rafi, sweetie, wake up," Sarah shook his shoulder gently. Rafi raised his head from where it was laying on his arm and looked around blearily. A red mark from his sleeve stood out on his otherwise pale cheek. For a moment he was disoriented. What was he doing sleeping in the basement?

His memory came flooding back with a rush, and he asked, "What time is it?"

"It's after midnight," his mother answered gently. "I went upstairs to check on the girls and came back to find you asleep. Go to bed, Rafi, you've done enough, really."

She pulled at his arm to get him to rise, but he resisted. His father, Jeff, and Tendall were standing over the reconfigured energy scanner, talking quietly. Every once in a while, one of them would make some small adjustment, and the others would examine the results.

"They've almost got it," Sarah said, following his gaze.

They were almost ready to scan for the twins. As tired as he was, he couldn't leave now. This was what they had been working toward all evening. To go to bed now while he knew all the important work was going on down here was just something he couldn't do. He had to stay; he had to see this through. He had to know the twins were still here.

"I want to stay," he told his mother. "I need to see if the scanner picks anything up." He willed her to understand what he couldn't say, the terrible fear that was nagging at his heart that maybe something really bad had happened, something that couldn't be reversed, and no matter what his mother said, he would consider himself responsible.

Sarah looked at him for a long moment. Then she nodded in consent and squeezed his shoulder, trying without speaking to communicate her thoughts.

We don't blame you; I wish you wouldn't blame yourself.

She had kept a concerned eye on him all throughout the long evening, watching him work with Jeff, respond to every order, fulfill every task set to him. It had seemed to her that this experience was making him grow up suddenly. As much as she hated to see him try to take responsibility for something that wasn't his fault, she was proud of the way he chose to join the rescue efforts when he had his tests to worry about, and the way he doggedly kept at it even though he was so tired.

"Alright," Chaim's voice broke into her reverie. "It's ready. With one machine we scan for the twins. It will relay the data to the other machine. We're looking for two very large concentrations of energy. Everyone ready?" He looked around at them all.

Heads nodded, and with a whispered prayer for help from Above, Chaim flipped a switch on one of the machines. It began to hum.

◆◆◆　◆　◆◆◆

"*Pssst*, Ahuva, wake up!" Elisheva whispered to her little sister. Ahuva rolled over in her sleep but didn't open her eyes.

Elisheva shook her shoulder gently. "Ahuva!" she hissed.

Ahuva opened her eyes blearily. "'Sheva?" she asked sleepily. "Whassa matter?"

"We need to help find Dovi and Dena," Elisheva whispered urgently. She could do it herself, but Ahuva had always been her loyal little sidekick. She felt more secure with Ahuva by her side.

Ahuva sat up in bed, rubbing her eyes with her chubby fists. "Ima said we can't help," she reminded her sister.

"I know," Elisheva admitted. "But we need to. If we don't, Dena and Dovi might be lost forever." She widened her eyes earnestly.

Ahuva thought about this. She distinctly re-membered her mother saying that the twins would come back, but what if Elisheva was right? Ahuva looked up to Elisheva as incredibly wise. After all, Elisheva went to first grade!

"Okay," she agreed finally. "What do we need to do?"

"Come with me," Elisheva beckoned, and Ahuva clambered out of bed. "Ima said the twins used Abba's machine and it turned them into energy, remember? And now they're stuck. We need to help change them back."

"Uh huh," Ahuva said, barely understanding what Elisheva was talking about. "How do we do that?"

"I'm not sure yet," Elisheva answered thoughtfully. "Do you have any ideas?" she asked hopefully.

"Nope," Ahuva shook her head.

Elisheva sighed. She'd have to think this through a little better. Meanwhile, the two nightgowned figures stole quietly down the hall and down the stairs. The house was dark and quiet, with shadows following them on the walls. Elisheva was suddenly glad Ahuva was with her. She didn't think she'd have the courage to do this otherwise.

"Where is everyone?" Ahuva whispered, coming closer to her sister.

"Probably in Abba's lab, trying to bring the twins back."

"'Sheva, if everyone else is trying to bring them back, why do we need to?" Ahuva asked.

"Because they don't know how," Elisheva answered as though this was obvious.

"But neither do we," Ahuva argued.

"*Shhh*," Elisheva held a finger to her lips. "I

think I have an idea. I heard Abba say they need a way to find where the twins are since they can't see them. So we can help them see them."

"How?" Ahuva wanted to know.

"Well, you know what energy is? You know how when Ima or Abba are very tired they say they have no energy, or they need to find some energy?"

"Yes," Ahuva affirmed. "And usually they say they can find energy if they get some sleep. So let's go to sleep!" She turned back toward her bedroom, but Elisheva grabbed her arm.

"Wait. Going to sleep isn't going to help."

"Eating?" Ahuva suggested hopefully.

"I don't think so. Eating or sleeping will just change us. We need to change the twins. It doesn't make so much sense; I can't quite figure it out."

"Maybe the twins need to eat," Ahuva said.

Elisheva's face brightened. "Yeah, I bet that would help. But because they're changed they can't find food."

"So what do we do?" Ahuva asked, her forehead puckered with concern.

A brilliant smile lit up Elisheva's features. "We feed them, of course!"

Tugging her sister's arm, they headed for the kitchen.

◆ ◆ ◆   ◆   ◆ ◆ ◆

"Wake up, Dena, they're doing it. Dena, they're searching for us," Dovi tugged on Dena's sleeve to wake her. When Dena saw that she wasn't able to stay awake any longer, Dovi had volunteered to keep watch while she slept. And this is what he had been waiting for. "Dena, get up!"

Dena heard her brother calling to her through a haze of fatigue. Forcing her brain back to consciousness, she opened her eyes.

"What?" she asked hoarsely, licking dry lips with an even drier tongue. She was so thirsty. She had been dreaming of a large glass of ice water. She had just been about to drink ….

"They're ready to use the energy scanner!" Dovi continued to tug at her insistently. He didn't appear to have slept at all. Not for the first time, Dena wondered where he got all his energy. He never seemed to run out.

She got to her feet, still trying to fully wake up. Her thirst wasn't helping. It was making it hard to concentrate. All she could think about was how badly she needed water.

Dena and Dovi stood side by side while their father began moving his sensor slowly around the room, pausing every few seconds while rows of numbers appeared in glowing red on the other screen. Jeff read them out and then Chaim moved the machine another few inches. It was slow and tedious work, and Dovi quickly became impatient with how long it was taking.

"Let's move," he suggested. "We can go closer to where Abba's using the sensor."

Dena was about to agree, but then she thought of something.

"I think we better stay where we are," she stopped her brother. "We might throw off Abba's readings if we move around."

Dovi opened his mouth to argue with her, but then changed his mind. They had waited this long, a few more minutes couldn't really hurt anything. And perhaps Dena was right; after all this waiting they couldn't risk messing things up.

After what seemed like an eternity to both children, the sensor in their father's hand turned in their direction. The twins held their breath and waited. The response was almost immediate. The sensor began beeping rapidly, its lights flashing, and Jeff, bent over the other sensor, muttered, "Whoa ..."

"What is it?" Chaim asked urgently. "What do you see?"

He kept his own sensor focused on the point

that had caused the reaction, right in front of the twins' noses. They could tell, though, that he was itching to examine the other sensor himself.

"The energy levels just jumped sky high," Jeff reported excitedly. "It's got to be one of the twins! I can't think of any other explanation for numbers this high."

The air was suddenly charged with excitement. The twins really were here! They were here even though no one could see or hear or touch them. It was unbelievable. Rafi gave an exclamation of relief. Chaim buried his face in one hand for a moment. Sarah began to cry softly.

"Record the number," Chaim instructed. His eyes were shining. Not only did they now know for sure that the twins were not somewhere out in the cold dark night, but they had just proven that his machine worked! Matter, a large amount of matter at that, had been successfully changed to energy. Wait until they told the board about this tomorrow.

But first things first.

Once Tendall confirmed that the number had been recorded, Chaim said, "Now we have to find the other twin."

He moved the monitor a few inches to the right. Once it was no longer aimed at the twins, the beeping slowed, finally stopping, and the light stopped flashing. Chaim waited a few seconds, and then moved again.

It took a few minutes before the reality of what was happening penetrated the twins' tired brains. When it did, they exchanged looks of horror.

"Oh, no," Dena moaned. "They read the energy and thought it was only one of us. What's going to happen when they don't find another large energy reading?" She couldn't believe she had been so thoughtless. And they had been so close!

15

"**W**HAT'LL WE FEED THEM?" Ahuva wanted to know, as they stood in the kitchen shivering in their bare feet.

Elisheva thought for a few minutes. "Something with the most energy," she decided.

"Breakfast?"

"Huh?"

"Ima always says a good breakfast gives you energy for the entire day," Ahuva insisted.

Elisheva nodded slowly. "You're right, she does. Good thinking," she praised her little sister.

They headed for the cabinet with the breakfast cereals, Elisheva's heart beating fast with excitement. They were really going to help find the twins! Everyone would be so proud of them when they found out.

She pushed away the uncomfortable little voice that reminded her that Ima had specifically told her she couldn't help, that she was to go to bed. Everyone was always treating her like a baby. It was time for them all to see that she could be useful too.

"Elisheva, what's this?" Ahuva's voice broke into her thoughts. She was pointing to a colorful box on the shelf.

Elisheva read the label. "Energy bars. Energy bars! Ahuva, do you know what we found?"

"Energy bars?" Ahuva guessed.

"The perfect food for the twins!" Elisheva exclaimed, pulling several plastic packets out of the box and beginning to open them.

"We'll spread them all over," Elisheva explained. "The twins will definitely find them. Crumble them into little pieces and spread them all over," Elisheva ordered, liking the feeling of being in command. "You do the kitchen and playroom. I'll do the living room and dining room. I'll meet you back in here when we're done, okay?"

Ahuva nodded agreeably and the two girls happily set about their task.

◆◆◆　◆　◆◆◆

Dovi racked his brains trying to come up with a solution to their newest problem.

"I'll move now," he finally suggested. "They'll read me again and consider that they got both of us."

Dena shook her head, her eyes filled with tears. She rarely cried, but she was so very tired!

"It won't work," she said glumly. "You will only register as half of what they got when they scanned both of us. Remember, they recorded the numbers. They'll consider it an anomaly. They won't think it's you." She started to slide back down to the floor in defeat, but Dovi grabbed her hand and pulled her back up.

"Then we'll both go to another place and let them read both of us again," he said, determined not to let Dena wallow in self-pity. When a solution presented itself it was time for action. And action was something Dovi excelled at.

She looked up at her brother, astonished that she had not thought of this solution herself, and then protested weakly, "We agreed we'd stay put so we don't mess up their readings." It was a token protest and she knew it.

Dovi rolled his eyes as he pulled her along behind him. "We want to mess with their readings, silly," he told her as they reached a part of the room that hadn't been scanned yet. They stood still as their father pointed the sensor at them yet again, with the same results as the last time.

The basement broke out in a spontaneous cheer. The men all shook hands and Sarah, wiping her eyes, hugged Rafi joyfully.

"That's both of them," Chaim confirmed unnecessarily. "They've both been here in the lab the entire time. This is great!"

He sank into his chair, his knees suddenly shaky in his relief. Jeff gave him an understanding smile and took the sensor from him, reading out the numbers to Tendall, who recorded them.

Jeff compared the two results and announced, "They're the same. Two huge concentrations of energy, two missing children. That's half the battle. But remember," he cautioned, "the most difficult part in all of this is still to come. The twins can't exist forever in a state of energy. We still have to find a way to change them back."

The atmosphere in the room sobered immediately.

"Forgive my ignorance in this area," Tendall spoke up, "but couldn't we just aim the machine at each concentration of energy and activate it again?"

Chaim and Jeff shook their heads in unison. Both "concentrations of energy" came closer to make sure they heard every word of this crucial matter.

"That won't work," Jeff explained. "The MEC was designed specifically to convert matter to energy and back, but we never got to the second part since we never succeeded at the first, which we in any case considered more important. And although the principle is similar, reversing it would require a whole new set of equations to be worked out." He switched off the sensor and laid it on the desk.

"And we have no margin for error," Chaim added. "Usually, these things are tested an inordinate amount of times on inanimate objects before moving on to living creatures, let alone human beings. If we're going to try this on the twins there can be no mistakes. Everything has to be balanced to the last decimal point. We can't do this by trial and error."

Sarah looked around at the little group. She had been so relieved when they had found the twins, but now, listening to her husband and his partner, her alarm grew. She wished she could press a magic button and make everything all right, but with a sinking feeling she realized that it might be a while before she saw her children again.

"How long will it take to work out all those equations?" she asked anxiously.

Chaim smiled at her, trying to be reassuring, but she could see that he too was worried.

"Thanks to Dena, we at least have a starting point," Chaim stated. "The balanced equation she used to change themselves in the first place. We'll work backwards from there."

The others all nodded readily, but Jeff regarded Chaim with a strange expression on his face. Chaim knew why: the complications involved in transforming Dena and Dovi back to matter were way more complex than he had let on. Chaim was aware of this but he had no wish to discourage his rather unlikely team of a teenager, a police officer, and a high school history teacher with more details than he felt they could handle.

Chaim caught Jeff's eye and held it, trying to silently communicate to him that he knew about the other problems, but thought it better not to mention them quite yet.

"One step at a time," he told his longtime friend and partner, his eyes speaking words his mouth wasn't saying. "Let's just get through this one step at a time."

Jeff returned his gaze for a long moment, then

nodded once and turned away. But Chaim had read the words in his eyes, "Message received."

As the men buckled down to work, Sarah went to refresh everyone's coffee. Coming up the stairs, she thought she heard a rustling noise in the kitchen and went to investigate.

"What's this?" she asked herself, feeling something crunch beneath her foot. In the dim light, she saw the kitchen floor was littered with crumbs!

How did this get here? she wondered. *I know I cleaned up after dinner!*

She switched on the overhead light to get a better look.

"Elisheva! Ahuva!" she exclaimed, seeing the two girls crouched by the stove, with deer-caught-in-headlights expressions on their faces. "What are you doing here?"

"Ima," Elisheva stammered. "We were just ..." Her voice trailed off.

"We were putting out food for the twins so they could find energy," Ahuva announced, pointing at the crumbs scattered about.

"What?! Oh, no," Sarah examined the package in Elisheva's hand. "Those bars are really expensive. And you crumbled them all over the floor? Elisheva, what were you thinking?" she asked sternly.

"That we wanted to help," Elisheva replied with a stubborn tilt of her head. "Everyone else gets to."

Sarah shook her head. This was not what she needed to be dealing with right now. She was about to scold some more when she caught sight of their downcast faces.

"I understand how much you want to help," she told them in a more gentle tone than she had been about to use. "But this is something the grown-ups need to take care of. You can help best right now by doing what you're told. Now get back to bed, right now, both of you. I'll sweep up in here."

Ahuva turned to go, but paused when her sister held back.

"Uh, Ima?" Elisheva said, tentatively. "It's also in the playroom, living room, and dining room. We wanted to make sure the twins could find it."

Sarah barely refrained from rolling her eyes in exasperation. "Okay, we'll finish cleaning it up to-morrow. Now, bed!"

She pointed toward the stairs and the two girls hurried away without a backward glance. Sarah leaned against the counter, suddenly overcome with a fit of laughter. Energy bars, of all things! What would they think of next?

When she had composed herself, she refilled

the cups and brought the coffee downstairs while Chaim brought up Dena's formula on the computer screen.

"Everything okay upstairs?" Chaim asked her. "I thought I heard voices."

"Just the girls," Sarah answered. "I'll tell you about it later."

They all turned their attention to the computer screen, at the long string of numbers and symbols that had started all this trouble. Tendall traced the equation with one long, lanky finger, trying to make sense of it. "You're sure this was a ten-year-old that fixed this thing?" he asked incredulously.

"Two ten-year-olds," Sarah corrected, pouring coffee into his cup. "And Dena has a gift for under-standing numbers."

"A gift!" Tendall repeated. "That has got to be one of the biggest understatements I've ever heard. I bet most physicists couldn't figure this out." He gestured again to the screen.

"A gift," Chaim stated firmly. "An intuitive understanding of math and physics. But don't fool yourself about what happened here, Officer. Dena acted with neither knowledge nor foresight. She saw an equation in front of her, an equation developed by others over a period of years. She saw an apparent flaw and corrected it. But she did it without any idea of what that equation meant, or what would be the consequences of her actions, leading to our current circumstances. Dena is very smart, there's no doubt about that. But brains like hers without learning, without self-control, without taking the time to understand, can be dangerous, as I'm sure she now realizes."

Dovi glanced at Dena as their father finished speaking. Her face was flushed red and her eyes were downcast. Dovi felt bad for her. His father's speech had been harsh, he felt. Dena was taking the rebuke hard.

Dovi wondered if Abba would have said all that if he knew Dena was listening when he realized with a start that Abba did know. He meant for Dena to hear what he had said. Dena was so rarely the subject of Abba's criticism she barely knew what it felt like. Having a much greater propensity for mischief, Dovi could definitely relate to what she was feeling now.

"It's okay," he told her quietly, wanting to make her feel better. "It's okay to make a mistake once in a while, Abba understands that. I make mistakes all the time. We both did something wrong, and when we're able to we'll apologize and that will be that. Don't be too hard on yourself."

Dena looked up at him, her eyes magnified by her tears. She heard what he was saying, but she had always prided herself on her self-discipline and her maturity. She had been delighted to have her father's admiration and respect. Now she felt she had lost all that with one thoughtless move. Would her father ever trust her again the way he had?

There was not much Tendall, Sarah, and Rafi could do now to help. Rafi eventually fell back into a half slumber, his head resting on his arm, his glasses askew. Sarah couldn't bring herself to sleep and she paced restlessly, and Tendall showed no sign of wanting to leave. So they split into two groups, each working on one side of the equation, Sarah double-checking Chaim's work, and Tendall double-checking Jeff's. After all, they were all tired, and by this time, prone to mistakes.

The time passed slowly. There was little talking. Fatigue began to pull at them, slowly but surely. First, Tendall began rubbing his eyes, and then Jeff got up for a brisk stroll around the lab. Sarah found her mind wandering, unable to focus anymore on the endless series of numbers. Chaim drank cup after cup of coffee, hot and black.

The twins both fell asleep. Every so often, one of them would jerk awake, quickly scan the lab, see that nothing had changed, and fall back to sleep.

It was just past three in the morning when Chaim and Jeff put the two sides of the equation together and compared them.

"It looks alright to me," Jeff offered wearily. "But we're all exhausted. Better run it through the computer simulations."

Chaim agreed, and began feeding the finished formula into the computer. The program took several minutes to run, and they all used the time to freshen up.

The computer beeped, letting them know that the program was complete. Jeff checked it.

"Looks like there are a couple inconsistencies, here, and here," he pointed.

"Okay," Chaim sighed, "let's go through it again."

The second time they ran it through the computer, no problems were found with the equation.

"That in itself is something of a miracle," Chaim told the relieved group. It had been dull work, very technical, difficult at the best of times, but especially hard in the middle of the night when they were all seriously craving sleep. Now they could finally move on.

"What now?" Tendall asked, his voice having

taken on a hoarse quality, betraying his exhaustion.

"Now we test it," Chaim answered, equally tired. The circles had deepened under his dark eyes, and his previously crisp white shirt was now wrinkled and stained. But he looked hardly worse than the rest of them as they prepared to test their work.

And here they came to the next set of problems. For one thing, every time they had tested the machine in the past, it overloaded. True, they had been trying to convert matter to energy, not the other way around, but neither Chaim nor Jeff could see why that should make much difference. Another difficulty lay in the pile of melted test objects they had tried to convert. They couldn't predict what would happen to the subject when it was rematerialized, but they couldn't risk the twins until they did.

Chaim and Jeff began to explain all this to their new lab partners. Sarah just shook her head, overwhelmed by all the information as well as by the magnitude of the task that lay before them. Even though she understood that they couldn't rush, that they couldn't risk making a mistake, she just wanted the twins back already, safe and sound in their own beds. She just wanted it to be all over.

Tendall rose with a resigned air. "Well, let's get

started," he prodded them. "What do we use for testing?"

"We could use anything really," Chaim said thoughtfully.

"As long as you don't plan to need it again," Jeff interjected dryly.

No one laughed; it wasn't really funny.

"We should try to use things that chemically most resemble human beings," Chaim continued as though Jeff hadn't spoken.

Tendall raised an eyebrow. "Do you have any pets?"

This time Chaim did laugh. "Just some gold-fish. But we're not going to use them. I meant something made of matter that also has its own energy source, like a human does; something not entirely inert."

They all gave this some thought, then scattered about the house to see what they could find that fit this criteria. Having had a specific goal, a job they knew they could do, had reenergized them all. When they were ready, they gathered in the lab once more to compare their finds.

Tendall had come up with a few batteries in various sizes. Chaim nodded approvingly and Tendall smiled, relieved that his contribution would be accepted. Jeff had brought a couple clocks and two wristwatches. Sarah had brought an electronic game. Chaim showed them a toy robot and a frozen chicken.

"A chicken?!" Sarah exclaimed.

"I thought it would be a good idea to try something organic," Chaim defended his choice with an exaggeratedly injured air. His aggrieved look caused everyone to chuckle.

"We'll start with the batteries," Chaim decided, "then the clocks, the watches, the game, the robot and the chicken, in order of increasing molecular complexity."

And so they began. Fortunately, the MEC didn't explode when they tried to convert the first battery; unfortunately, the battery exploded. They all ducked as pieces went flying.

"Sheesh," Tendall commented, raising his head cautiously. "You weren't kidding about this thing still having some bugs to work out."

Sarah pulled on some thick rubber gloves and picked up the scattered battery pieces as Jeff and Chaim made some minute adjustments to the machine. Tendall recorded the settings, so they wouldn't try the same ones twice.

They tried again. This caused a meltdown in

the computer wires. Sarah turned on a fan to help clear out the powerful smell as well as all the smoke, and Tendall brought a new set of wires from the supply shelf. As Chaim replaced the wires again, he commented wryly, "I lost count of how many times I've done this already today. Pretty soon I'll be able to do it with my eyes closed."

And they tried again. And again. Each time something went wrong. The mood had started out ebullient, charged with excitement. With each failure to produce the desired results, the spirits of the valiant little group fell lower.

Eventually they ran out of batteries and decided to move on to the clocks. Chaim reset the computer for the tenth time while the others sat around glumly, lost in thought. Rafi had awakened, and joined the others around the MEC.

"This is the problem we've been having this whole time," Jeff pointed out. "The only way for the machine to work is to balance the equation like Dena did, and fry the MEC in the process."

Chaim wasn't convinced. "What if we tried to insulate the MEC's components better? Make it able to tolerate higher levels of energy?"

"We've tried that," Jeff reminded him. "We never found a material strong enough."

They fell silent again, both wracking their brains in an effort to solve a problem that didn't seem to have a solution.

When the computer was ready, they began again. But the best they were able to do was cause the clocks to phase slightly, turning somewhat transparent. Any more energy and the MEC blew. All the activity had also awakened the twins, and they hovered around, watching the proceedings.

"What is it?" Dovi asked, almost to himself. "What are they doing wrong?"

"I don't know," Dena answered, rubbing her eyes, which felt gritty and heavy.

"This isn't working," Chaim finally declared. "We must be going about this the wrong way."

Sarah sighed, her shoulders slumping. "Chaim, we're doing everything we can think of. What else is there?" Her voice was tinged with panic.

In a few hours it would be daylight. Somehow, in her mind, the morning had become their time limit. At some point, she would have to go wake up the girls, get them dressed and fed, and get Rafi and Elisheva out the door. She would have to arrange for a substitute since she would be in no condition to teach, having been up all night. But how could she do any of those mundane things if the twins hadn't been saved yet? For that matter, how would Rafi manage throughout the day? Maybe he should just stay home and make up the test later. She knew how he felt about seeing this through.

Jeff stood up and started to pace in front of the MEC thinking out loud as he walked.

"The machine worked on the twins, and melted the computer down in the process. We know it didn't destroy them because they were able to communicate. In order to test the machine in reverse, we first need to transform an inanimate object so that we can bring it back. There's no help for it. We're going to have to increase the energy, transform something, and melt the MEC."

He stopped pacing and looked at Chaim. "It's the only way. You know that. We need to use the same equation Dena used."

16

CHAIM SHOOK HIS HEAD SLOWLY at his friend's words, while Dena cried futilely, "Listen to him, Abba! He's right!"

"If we burn out the machine on tests, how will we use it on the twins?" Chaim argued.

"We'll just have to repair it each time," Jeff answered, shrugging his broad shoulders.

"Every time?" Sarah repeated in despair. "That'll take forever!"

"Not to mention that we'll run out of parts long before we're ready to bring back the twins," Chaim added. He went over to his supply shelves, and rapidly rifled through the reserves, doing quick mental calculations as he did. "In fact, I've used so much today I'm already running low."

Jeff joined him at the shelves to see for himself. It was true, they were running low on several essential components. Jeff felt a pang. He wanted so badly to help his friend get his children back safely. And at the same time he couldn't forget that the relentless ticking of the clock brought them ever closer to the time their fellow company members were expecting a demonstration of MEC's capabilities.

How ironic, Jeff thought, *that we have the proof that the machine can work right here in this room, and we can't tell anyone.*

After a long moment during which no one spoke, Chaim finally came to a decision.

"We'll go with Jeff's idea," he announced. "We'll deal with the spare parts issue when we come to it."

That settled it, and everyone buckled down again to work. Dena gave an exclamation of relief, and Dovi stared at her curiously.

"Why was that so important to you?" he wanted to know.

"Because," Dena answered as though it were obvious, "that's the only way the machine will work."

Dovi scrutinized the machine with a puzzled look on his face, as though he would find the answers to his questions written out for him there.

"How do you figure that?" he asked, apparently failing to find anything of value in the MEC.

Dena shrugged uncomfortably. "I really can't explain it," she admitted. "It's just a strong feeling I have. I see the numbers so clearly in my head, I see how they have to be, but I don't really understand why or —" She broke off, shaking her head, frustrated by her inability to put into words something that was so clear in her mind.

Dovi gazed at her quietly for a few seconds. "Has anyone ever told you that you are unbelievable sometimes?" he asked wonderingly.

Dena gave a soft laugh of appreciation. "I seem to recall hearing it a couple times," she acknowledged. She waited a moment, trying to verbalize what she felt. She didn't always have the easiest time expressing herself, but she felt there was something important she had to say.

"Dovi," her voice was hesitant, almost shy. "You've been really amazing through all of this. I don't know what I would have done if I was going through this alone ...." her voice trailed off, but Dovi flashed her a glance of appreciation, his face lacking its usual expression of mischief.

"Thanks for saying that," he said softly. "You've been pretty amazing yourself."

The moment was interrupted by the rising whine of the MEC and gasps from the onlookers. Dena and Dovi watched as the clock became steadily more transparent until it faded from view. Before it completely faded, the computer began emitting sparks. Jeff placed his hands, sheathed in protective rubber gloves, over the wires attaching the MEC to its computer. The second the battery became invisible, Jeff yanked the wires out of the machine and let out a triumphant whoop.

Breathlessly, Chaim checked the readout on the side of the MEC.

"The amount of energy inside the energy capacitor is at .3 percent!" he exclaimed. "The MEC is containing the energy just as it's supposed to." His tone was exultant. For the first time, he had seen the work of the past three years bear fruit. He turned to Jeff who was examining the wires in his hands. "How bad is the damage?" he asked anxiously.

"Minimal," Jeff replied, every bit as exhilarated as his friend. "I think I got them out in time. These connectors should be good for another go."

"The computer is a little worse for the wear, but it's still functional," Tendall reported, straightening up and stretching. "And I have to tell you that is one of the more incredible things I've ever seen. Congratulations!"

"We ought to open a bottle of champagne and make a toast to three years' work!" Jeff enthused, beaming around at everyone, fatigue forgotten.

The twins stared at the place where the clock had been a moment before.

"Whoa!" Dovi murmured, shaken. "That's what happened to us!"

Dena nodded, her eyes wide with awe and wonder.

"But where is it?" Dovi wondered, looking around as though searching for something.

"Where is what?" Dena asked, distracted.

"The clock," Dovi said insistently, trying to get her attention.

She wrinkled her forehead to show her confusion at his question.

"We're energy, and we're here. We can see each other. Now the clock is energy too, where is it? Why can't we see it?" Dovi was very worried that this meant something had gone wrong with the transformation.

However, Dena's face cleared, her confusion fading. She smiled. "We can't see the clock because it's being stored inside the converter, just like the machine was designed to do," she explained.

"And we're not being stored inside the converter?" Dovi already knew the answer to that, but Dena shook her head anyway.

"Then," Dovi completed his thought, "how are they going to transform us back?"

Dena just stared at him wordlessly. She didn't know the answer to his question, but she was confident they would figure something out. There was no other choice.

The group had progressed to testing the MEC on the watches. This was not much more complicated than the clocks, and was accomplished without too much difficulty. At this point they paused to replace several burned out components, and repair what they could of the MEC. It was clear that every time they used the machine it took a great toll on the technology involved. But after each transformation, a greater amount of energy was recorded as being stored.

"Why is this working?" Sarah asked. "I thought every time you tried it this way you practically destroyed that machine." She indicated the MEC.

"It must have something to do with these things all having their own energy source and the things we used previously didn't," Chaim answered. "I'm not sure why that makes a difference, but clearly, it does."

"At least we know the energy storage unit works well," Jeff said encouragingly after they transformed the toy computer. "I see no sign of instability."

Sarah glanced at one of the basement's small rectangular windows. It was nearly five o'clock in the morning, though the sky outside was still dark. The clouds had blown away and she could see the stars, a hundred glittering diamonds on an ocean of black. But she couldn't let the darkness outside deceive her; morning had nearly arrived.

Rafi was positioning the little grey robot in front of the MEC, according to his father's instructions. Sarah went over to him and decisively removed the robot from his hands. They all regarded her curiously.

"Enough of this," she said tersely. "We know the transformer works, at least to a certain degree. Now I want you to bring something back. I need to know that we can bring the twins back." Her tone brooked no argument.

Sarah was well aware of how long her husband and Jeff had been waiting for results like these, and how much it meant to them that they had finally achieved a large measure of success, but she couldn't have them lose sight of what was important here. The only reason they were transforming inanimate objects was in order to test their ability to bring back the twins. Scientific advancement aside, the end result was the only thing that mattered right now.

Chaim and Jeff exchanged a long glance, while Tendall and Rafi maintained carefully blank expressions. Jeff gave a minute nod.

"Alright," Chaim agreed. "We'll put off testing the rest of these for now. But remember, just like transforming from matter to energy gets more difficult the more complex the object, changing back is the same way. We'll want to test the most complex things we have before trying it on the twins."

"I understand," Sarah told him. "Please, bring back the computer."

To her disappointment, it wasn't immediately possible. First, the proper pattern had to be localized within the storage unit. Then they had to input that data, together with the equation they had reversed, into the computer. Finally, after what seemed like an eternity to the anxious mother, they were ready.

Sarah held her breath and waited, davening the whole time, her hands gripping the back of a chair until her knuckles turned white. Jeff carefully pushed up the lever while Chaim continually input new data in response to Tendall's voice, as he was reading off the changing numbers on the monitor.

Sarah and Rafi were staring at the spot from where the computer had recently vanished, as though the force of their gaze could cause it to reappear.

"Something's happening!" Rafi exclaimed excitedly, spotting a small, circular pattern of matter floating in the air.

Something was indeed happening. The matter began to take on clearer form and substance, but then the lights began to flicker. There was a short break in the continuous whine of the working machine, which changed in pitch until it was more of a shriek, then another, longer break in the noise. Smoke rose from the MEC's control panel.

"Shut it down," Chaim yelled, typing frantically on his keyboard. "Now, before it destroys itself!"

Jeff yanked out several wires with a grimace of dismay. Tendall pulled several more out of the wall and the machine went silent. For a long moment nothing moved except the wisps of smoke still rising from the MEC. The incandescent particles had disappeared.

"Well, that was certainly a disaster," Tendall said conversationally, but his grey eyes were somber.

"I'll say," Jeff seconded emphatically.

"Guess it's a good thing we did some trial runs instead of testing it on the twins first," Rafi murmured to his mother.

"What happened?" Sarah demanded. "What went wrong?" Her face was white.

There was a pause as Jeff and Chaim examined the data. Dena and Dovi waited tensely to hear the answer. They could tell this latest setback was not good news.

"It takes more power than the equipment can handle," Jeff finally concluded. "Same problem we've been having all along, only in reverse." He sat on the edge of the table, his broad shoulders slumping in exhaustion as the adrenalin caused by the last few minutes drained away.

"But we were able to make the things disappear, why shouldn't we be able to bring them back?" Rafi wanted to know.

"Well, the energy requirements —" Jeff began to explain but Sarah interrupted him.

"I'm sure it's a very important question and I'm sure there's a very good answer, but right now I want to know what you're going to do about it. Please," she implored, "we're running out of time."

"Okay," Chaim said rubbing his forehead, trying to think. "We need to increase the machine's energy capacitor. It's the only way. If we can't do that, we're just wasting our time. So think, everyone, think. How can we enable the machine to allow more energy flow? Think," he insisted, as though they weren't already wracking their brains.

It was finally Tendall who spoke up, tentatively, "What if we freeze it?"

The others turned to stare at him.

"What?" Jeff asked.

"Well, I'm no physicist," Tendall began to explain. "But I know that when something freezes, the movement of the particles inside it slows and its energy level decreases. I just thought maybe if you froze the parts of your machine, maybe it wouldn't burn out as fast," he finished, somewhat uncertainly. "Sorry if that didn't make any sense," he apologized. "I'm a little out of my league here."

Chaim and Jeff gazed appreciatively at the officer. Over the hours that they had spent together, they had come to admire and respect the man who had volunteered to work with them, though he had no obligation to. They had learned much about the reticent officer over the long and difficult night. They knew that Tendall was thoughtful and intelligent and soft-spoken. They were glad that he had spoken up now.

"Why didn't we ever think of that before?" Chaim asked Jeff, who just shook his head.

"Sometimes the best answer is the simplest. We may have been over-thinking things a little," Jeff acknowledged.

"You mean you think it might work?" Tendall asked, surprised.

"I think it will help," Chaim answered, moderating, and Jeff murmured his agreement. "But I don't think it will be quite enough. It's a good start, though."

He began selecting certain components of the MEC and removing them. After a second, Jeff moved in to help him.

"What are you doing?" Sarah asked.

"Picking the parts to freeze," her husband told her. Then he added, jokingly, "Should we put them in the freezer, or just stick them outside?"

Jeff peeked at the thermostat by the door and answered seriously, "Considering that the temperature outside is at minus three degrees, I'd say outside would be a better bet."

"You got it," Chaim agreed and together they brought the parts they had removed to the door and placed them carefully outside in the snow.

"They'll need a little time to freeze," Chaim pointed out, and Sarah made an impatient sound. "But we won't waste that time. Meanwhile, we should be getting every bit of insulation for every part of the machine as we can. Maybe these two strategies together will be effective long enough to bring back the twins."

"What kind of insulation should we be looking for?" Rafi wanted to know.

"Rubber," his father told him. "All of the rubber we can get our hands on."

So once more they spread throughout the house, this time on a quest for the material that might keep the MEC components from melting down the next time it was used. Jeff was the only one not joining the hunt, as he used the time to repair the damage done during their first attempt at energy-matter conversion.

By the time they all gathered again, streaks of light had appeared in the sky, brilliant colors of pink, purple, yellow, and red. The world outside was brightening with every passing moment. Soon its inhabitants would begin to stir, rising to start a brand new day, a day of hope and promise. What would their new day bring?

Chaim retrieved the now frozen computer parts, and he and Jeff swiftly began installing them, wrapping everything in layers of insulating rubber.

"We have to work quickly," Chaim explained as Tendall handed him the rubber sole of an old shoe. "Before the parts defrost."

Rafi gave Jeff a pair of his mother's rubber gardening gloves. "Do you think we found enough?" he asked, indicating the pile they had collected.

"Let's hope so," his father replied, using a knife to cut up a rubber rain boot.

While the men were working on the repairs and insulation, Sarah was re-isolating the energy pattern in the storage unit. She had seen her husband and Jeff do it the last time, and she was quite sure she remembered how. Every so often, however, she got stuck and asked Chaim to talk her through it.

More quickly than seemed possible, they were ready.

"Let's bring back that computer," Chaim said, his face set in determined lines. It couldn't fail this time. He whispered a quick prayer: *Please, Hashem, let this work; help me save my children.* Jeff overheard Chaim's words. He looked over and saw that Sarah had opened a Tehillim and was reading from it intently. She wasn't even watching the test. Jeff added his own plea to those of his friends.

Please, G-d, help us save those children!

Once again, Jeff pulled the lever while Chaim continually input data, trying to keep everything in control.

"0.4, 0.5," Tendall read from the monitor and Chaim listened with half an ear, keeping his adjustments in sync with the officer's words.

"Steady," he murmured to Jeff as the whine began to change in pitch. "Slow and steady. Give it time to adjust."

Rafi again spotted the floating haze of particles, just as the numbers Tendall was reading began to go in the other direction, "0.4, 0.3 ..."

"It's working!" Rafi exclaimed in delight, and although the machine was smoking and an oppressive heat was emanating from it, he could see the outline of the computer taking clearer form, and then increasing in solidity, resting on the stool from which it had disappeared several hours previously.

".0001 ... zero!" Tendall said, and immediately Chaim and Jeff cried out together, "Shut it down!"

The shrieking whine faded to silence. For a second, no one dared breathe, and then Sarah went and picked up the computer, turning it over in her hands. "It's here," she whispered. "I can see it. I can *feel* it."

Chaim and Jeff both appeared to be stunned. "I can't believe this," Jeff shook his head in wonder. "How did that happen?"

"What do you mean?" Tendall asked, puzzled. "Isn't this what you were expecting to happen?"

The two scientists looked at each other.

"It shouldn't have worked," Chaim admitted flatly.

"We tried it out of desperation. It doesn't make any sense," Jeff added.

Sarah was smiling, for the first time in what felt like a long time. "You'll figure out why it worked another time," she told them gently. "Now let's use it on the twins."

Chaim didn't say anything for a long moment. "You realize, of course, that the twins are way more complex, and are much larger than that computer." He was afraid that just because, by some fluke, the machine had worked once, it wouldn't necessarily happen again.

"What if you bring them back one at a time?" Tendall suggested.

Chaim seemed to consider it, but Jeff shook his head. "It's too risky. Look at the damage using the machine this way has caused. If the machine breaks down with the first transfer and we can't get it fixed in time, the other twin would be stuck."

"But if you overload the machine trying to bring back both of them at the same time, you may not get either one," Tendall argued.

"The energy required to bring two at the same time is less in total than that required to operate the machine twice at such intense levels." Jeff insisted. "Not only that, but how could we be sure we were separating their patterns properly? After all, they're just wandering around; they're not stored in the machine the way the clock was."

Chaim nodded slowly, convinced. "We do both at the same time," he decided, and Tendall dipped his head in graceful concession. "We have to make sure the activation beam is focused at the twins' location." He stopped, thinking.

This wasn't as simple as changing back the computer. The fact that was twins were wandering free, uncontained, severely complicated matters. They had to make sure that they transformed all of each twin; he didn't want to think what would happen if they accidentally left part of them as energy. Was that even possible?

The seriousness of the danger to his children hit him with the force of a sledgehammer. With a groan of despair, he sank into a chair, his head in his hands. The other gathered around, wondering what was wrong.

"We can't do this," Chaim whispered to them without looking up. "It's too dangerous. There's too much that can go wrong ...." His voice trailed off hopelessly.

"Chaim, there's no choice, we have to try," Jeff offered, not knowing what else to say to comfort his friend.

"We'll be as careful as we can," Tendall added, trying to be reassuring.

Chaim just shook his head sadly.

Then Rafi went up to him and put his hand on his father's shoulder.

"Abba," he said quietly, and Chaim looked up at the boy as though seeing him for the first time. Where was the child he had known, and who was this young man standing in his place? With a start, he realized how hard this night must have been for his son.

"Abba, if anyone can do this, you can," Rafi said with complete and sincere faith in his father. "And if you can't, no one can. But, *b'ezras Hashem*, I think you can."

Chaim grasped the boy's hand tightly. How he admired his son in that moment. He could see how Rafi set aside his own guilt and fear to help his father deal with his. He let his pride in his son reflect on his face until he was sure Rafi saw and understood what he was feeling.

"Thank you, Rafi," he said quietly, "for your confidence in me."

He released the boy's hand and stood up, facing the others. His momentary despair had lifted and determination and hope blazed in his eyes.

"With G-d's help, let's bring the twins back to us."

"Uh, Chaim, I think we have a problem," Jeff announced unhappily. He was working with Tendall, holding the modified sensor, scanning for the twins' energy presence.

Chaim glanced up from the computer screen, where he was recalibrating the equations to the twin's energy levels. "What else is new?" he asked wearily, as he shook his head and sighed. "Sorry," he offered. "What is it?"

Jeff moved his sensor around the room again and glanced back at Tendall for confirmation. Tendall gave a slight, apologetic shake of his head.

"I can only pick up the energy signature for one twin," Jeff answered Chaim. "It's in the location of the second one we picked up. I've gone over the whole room, and I can't find the other one at all!"

At hearing this, Dena gave Dovi an angry look. "Now see what you've done!" she accused him.

"What are you talking about?" Dovi asked defensively. "What did I do?" He honestly couldn't figure out what his sister was talking about.

"You let them think both of us are one person, and now they think one of us is unaccounted for!" Dena paced agitatedly in front of her brother, two steps forward, turn, two steps back. Dovi wished she would stop; she was making him dizzy.

"So let's move again," Dovi suggested, as he had before, but even as he spoke he realized why that wouldn't work. "They're looking to have both of us in front of the beam at the same time. Whatever we do, we'll only register as half of what they're expecting," he answered himself before Dena could.

Dena nodded. "That's right," she agreed, but more calmly now that she saw he understood the problem. "So what do we do?"

Dovi thought hard, and then suddenly came to what he felt was the only reasonable course of action.

"We separate," he said, and began to move away from his sister.

Jeff, staring at his sensor, gave a sudden yelp.

Rafi, who was under the computer table installing more insulation, raised his head in surprise and banged it on the tabletop.

"Ow!" he complained, rubbing the top of his head.

Jeff frantically examined his sensor, then handed it to Sarah to hold in position while he ran to check the other sensor, looking over Tendall's shoulder.

"What?" Chaim demanded, not wanting to be kept in the dark.

"The pattern is destabilizing!" Jeff exclaimed, tracing the readout on the screen with his index finger. "It's losing molecular cohesion!"

Chaim abandoned his calculations and went to examine the tiny screen for himself. "We can't wait any longer," he decided. "We're going to go with Officer Tendall's idea by default. Activate the MEC," he ordered. "We're bringing this twin back now."

They all hurried to take their places. Chaim was still in the middle of calibrating equations on the computer and he resumed that task, and Jeff was holding onto the lever, controlling the rate of energy transfer. Tendall was reporting from the monitor, and Sarah and Rafi were holding the two small sensors wide apart, with the massive energy reading between them. This would focus the transfer beam and make sure the entire twin was transformed back. They both had to be extremely vigilant to make sure that the entire energy field was between their two sensors.

"Begin energy build-up," Chaim ordered, completing the final phase of his calculations.

"Beginning buildup," Jeff replied crisply, all business now that the crucial moment had arrived.

Tendall read aloud the changing numbers appearing on his screen. Chaim adjusted his programming to compensate for the increasing energy flow. They worked together like a well-oiled machine. They worked together as though they had always done so and always would. They worked with trust in each other, confident they would each perform their assigned task to the best of their abilities.

Sarah kept her eyes on her own screen, but her heart and mind were filled with prayer. *Please Hashem, bring my children back safely.* She couldn't think of anything more eloquent; she just repeated that one sentence over and over again.

Dovi and Dena stood together, not moving. They braced themselves for the change, waiting expectantly. They held each other's gazes and tried to speak without words, offering what support and encouragement they could. If they were frightened by what might happen, they didn't show it. There was no time for that now.

The now familiar whine began to build in intensity. The bright red light enveloped the twins, and they covered their eyes protectively. The heat began to build, reaching almost unbearable levels. The twins could not have moved even if they had been inclined to. They stood rooted to the spot.

Rafi looked up from his sensor to see the field of red light in front of him. The brilliance of it prevented him from peering into it for more than a moment, but in that instant he was almost sure he saw the outline of a figure ....

"Rafi, watch your sensor!" Jeff said sharply, seeing the boy lose focus and begin to move forward, heedless of the energy field he was supposed to be surrounding.

Rafi's attention snapped back to his screen, appalled at what he had nearly done. He expected rebuke, but no one said anything else about his lapse.

"The energy levels are nearing those at which the computer transformed," Tendall reported, mercifully removing the attention from the embarrassed boy. He had to speak loudly to be heard over the high-pitched shriek of the straining machine.

Jeff continued to push up the lever, slowly and steadily. "We need to go a whole lot higher than that this time," he reminded them loudly. "Stay with it, we're not even halfway there."

The temperature in the room began to climb, but no one could spare even a moment to wipe a sweaty forehead, much less remove a sweater. The light started to flicker, and Jeff, who was closest to the MEC mainframe, started to cough from the smoke rising from the machine. Soon they were all coughing.

"Keep it going," Jeff encouraged, his throat irritated and his eyes watering from the smoke. "Just a little further."

With his free hand, he wrapped a strip cut from a rubber potholder around a critical component, trying to keep the machine together long enough to complete this one last task.

"Come on," he murmured to the machine. "You can do it. Just hold together."

Tendall began to pant from the heat. "If you told me we were in the Sahara desert in the middle of July instead of North America in the middle of January, I would believe you at this point," he gasped, trying to lighten the mood, and reassure the others, who were giving him concerned looks.

His comment drew some small smiles.

"I'm reaching capacity," Jeff yelled over the noise a moment later. "That's all there is. I can't go any higher." He removed his hand from the now useless lever, picked up a few ice packs and placed them strategically over the MEC.

"Is it enough?" Sarah yelled back, without moving her sensor an inch. "Is there enough energy for them to transform?"

No one answered. Jeff was replacing burned out parts as quickly as his hands could move. Tendall suddenly called out, "The energy in the field is going down! The number is going down!" He jumped to his feet in excitement, but kept his eyes on his screen.

"What does that mean?" Sarah asked, her throat raw from heat and from tension.

"It means the transformation has started," Chaim answered. His calculations complete, he was helping Jeff trying to keep the MEC from disintegrating around them. "Keep davening! Just pray there's enough energy for them to complete the transformation."

Tendall continued to read off the numbers, his voice rising as the numbers got lower and lower. The lab was so suffused with the blazing crimson light that they could barely see and he had to put his face right near the screen in order to read off the numbers.

The MEC burst into flame. Chaim ran to the door and wrenched it open, but the blast of cold air barely put a dent into the sauna the lab had become. Chaim grabbed his lab's fire extinguisher and let it spray onto the flames, causing them to sizzle and sputter, but finally go out. At that same moment, he faintly heard Tendall's voice say, "… zero."

Jeff pulled several plugs out of the wall. Chaim pushed the lever all the way back down and flipped several switches into the off position. A detached corner of his mind noted that they had lost power from the backup generator.

The noise died down. The artificial luminescence faded. The oppressive heat receded. And there in front of them, bathed in the light of the new morning sun, stood two dirty, tired, bedraggled children.

There was a moment of incredulous silence, and then a cry of joy and wonder. Sarah ran forward, her arms outstretched, but stopped just short of touching the twins. She was afraid, suddenly, that she had fallen asleep and was dreaming, that if she actually tried to touch her children they would fade away from her, beyond her reach.

"Dovi?" she whispered. "Dena?"

"Ima?" Dovi returned, staring at her intently. "You can see us?"

Sarah nodded, too overcome to speak.

Dovi began to jump up and down, fatigue forgotten. "We're back! We're back!" he yelled, unable to stand still and contain his relief.

An exhausted Dena fell into her mother's embrace and burst into tears. Sarah held her, stroking her disheveled hair and murmuring reassurances.

The others gathered in closer around the twins. Chaim grabbed Dovi's hand and pulled him into a hug.

"You really are back," he agreed, his eyes overly bright. "*Baruch Hashem!*"

Jeff surveyed both children with a critical eye. "Well, you both look like you've been through the wringer," he said, his casual tone belying his joy at seeing the twins safe and sound.

"Are you both okay?" Sarah asked, pushing Dena away from her slightly so she could examine the children from head to foot. "You're not hurt?"

"We're fine," Dena answered, calm again, her eyes shining. They really were fine!

"Just very hungry," Dovi continued, rolling his eyes dramatically.

"And very thirsty," Dena added, feeling it difficult to speak through her parched throat.

"We're all thirsty," Rafi put in, not even beginning to know how to deal with his feelings at the return of his brother and sister. His relief was so staggering he thought it would overwhelm him.

"Let's get everyone upstairs and we'll get some drinks," Sarah said briskly, ushering them to the stairs.

At that moment they heard a soft beep, beep, beep. They all looked around, trying to trace its source.

Chaim held up his hand, showing his wristwatch. "It's seven o'clock," he announced. "Good morning, everyone, time to get ready for Shacharis!"

They all laughed and trooped upstairs.

Sitting together in the kitchen sipping cups of cold orange juice, the mood turned contemplative. They had all changed over the course of that very long night; changed in a way that was very real, for all that it was undefined.

They had learned something from the experience, each of them. Chaim learned the power of having someone believe in him, and hoped he could remember to pass that onward. Jeff had learned trust; he had reluctantly accepted Officer Tendall into his inner circle and had come to regard the older man as a friend. They stood together now, leaning against the kitchen counter, talking quietly.

"What made you decide to stay?" Jeff asked curiously. "You had no obligation to do that."

"I know," Tendall acknowledged, shrugging. "But I felt it was the right thing to do. I was very impressed with what I had seen here earlier and I wanted to help if I could. It's not every day you get a chance to be involved in an experience like this one."

Jeff had to acknowledge the truth of that statement.

"You seem very thoughtful," Chaim commented to Rafi, wanting to know what was going on inside his son's mind.

Rafi nodded slowly. Over the long night, he had seen the value of hard work and commitment; he had watched the adults plow forward and succeed against all odds. They had never given up, no matter what obstacles were thrown in their way.

"I guess I'm just trying to process everything," he answered noncommittally, and his father nodded his understanding.

Sarah sat between the twins now, afraid to take her eyes off them.

"You must have been very scared when you realized what happened," she said to them sympathetically.

"We were pretty worried," Dena admitted. "It took a while before we even figured out what did happen."

"We thought we might be stuck like that forever," Dovi said, rubbing his soot-smudged face. "Dena wasn't sure the machine would work in reverse."

"Well, no one was really sure, were they?" Dena defended herself, but her words lacked heat.

Dena had gotten a big dose of humility; she realized now how much she still had to learn, how many mistakes she had made that day. And she had learned that it was okay to make mistakes, because that was how one gained wisdom.

"I thought we might starve," Dovi added, reaching for one of the leftover cookies and munching on it hungrily. Dovi had also learned important things that night. He had learned that book knowledge had an important function in life. He had learned that it was okay to depend on someone else, sometimes, but he also had to be able to stand on his own two feet. And he had learned that if he missed a few meals, he would survive.

They spoke a little more, quietly, sleepily.

Both twins turned to their father now. "I'm really sorry for all the trouble I caused, Abba," Dena said, sincerely apologizing. She was grateful she was getting the chance.

"Me too," Dovi added quickly. "It was mostly my fault anyway."

Their parents exchanged glances, eyebrows raised. Dovi was voluntarily taking responsibility for something? Things really had changed.

"You're both responsible," Chaim told them. "But we'll talk about it later. Right now, I want both of you to go wash up and get some rest."

Not at all inclined to argue, the twins murmured another round of thanks to the group that had put in so much effort on their behalf and hurried out of the kitchen.

"And you," Chaim turned to Rafi. "What time is your first exam?"

"Ten o'clock, Gemara," Rafi answered stifling a yawn. "And I have my math exam at two." His face fell a little at the thought.

His father noticed.

"Go get some rest now," Chaim told him. "Ima will take you to school at nine thirty for *minyan* and your test. Hopefully at one o'clock I'll be able to go over your math with you."

211

Rafi gave him a grateful, tired smile. "Thank you, Abba," he said, and off he went to get what sleep he could.

Officer Tendall cleared his throat. "Seeing how everything worked out in the end, it's really time for me to be going. This has been some night." He shook his head, still amazed at everything he had witnessed that night. "Best of luck with your demonstration," he wished them, shaking hands with Chaim and Jeff. "If you ever need anything, let me know."

Chaim grasped the police officer's hand in a gesture of friendship. "I don't know how to thank you for everything," he told Tendall, knowing words were not enough to convey his gratitude. Sarah, too, offered her profuse thanks.

Tendall's retiring nature was uncomfortable with the attention. He raised his hand in farewell and took his leave of this remarkable family that had made such an impression on him. He felt, deep in his heart, that someday their paths would cross again.

CHAIM STOOD IN THE CENTER of his lab and surveyed the damage, Jeff at his side.

"It's quite a mess," Jeff noted, coming off the high he had experienced following the return of the twins. "We have a demonstration scheduled in four and a half hours, and we're both exhausted. That's not a recipe for a good outcome."

Chaim could hardly disagree. He turned in a slow circle, taking in the effect of the previous night on his formerly sovereign territory.

The tables were littered with used coffee cups, the floor sprinkled with cookie crumbs. Pieces of batteries, melted wires, and burned out computer parts were scattered across the room. The MEC itself was little more than a burned mass of metal and electrical pieces, sitting in puddles of fire extinguisher foam.

"We need to fix it," Chaim said softly, fingering the machine and looking at his soot-covered finger. "Quickly."

Jeff groaned in response.

"Chaim, seriously? We're ready to drop! We'll explain to the board that there was an emergency and ask to have the demonstration postponed to tomorrow. It's the only way," Jeff reasoned. "We don't even have all the parts we need to really repair the thing."

Chaim considered his friend's words. Jeff had logic on his side, no doubt. But Chaim found himself resisting this course of events. They had waited so long, worked so hard, and most of all, they had the proof in front of their own eyes that their efforts had paid off.

"Can you stand that?" he asked without looking at Jeff. "Being pushed off again?"

Jeff didn't answer for a moment. Chaim absently began to collect the coffee mugs onto the tray and sweep the crumbs from the table into his palm. Jeff thoughtfully pulled rubber pieces of insulation off the MEC.

"I don't know," he answered finally. "Everything we've gone through last night has made me see a few things. The project is important, that's true. But there are other things that are more important."

He put down the parts he was holding and went over to his friend.

"Let it go," he said quietly, intently. "Rest, help your son with his math. This will still be here tomorrow. And who knows, we might even do better if we have a few hours of sleep." He gave a weary chuckle.

Chaim smiled as well. "You're right, as usual," he conceded. "We'll postpone until tomorrow."

Jeff nodded, putting on his coat. "I'm going home now to rest, but I'll be back later to help you clean all this up and make repairs. Oh, and I'll take care of arranging the postponement."

Chaim thanked him and watched his friend leave, shutting the door behind him. For a moment longer he stood alone in his lab, and then he turned to go get some seriously needed and well-earned sleep.

♦♦♦　◆　♦♦♦

Dena snuggled under her blankets, reveling in their warmth and softness.

The room was quiet. As soon as her sisters had awakened, Ima had hurried them out of the room, explaining in hushed tones that Dena was tired and needed to rest. Of course, both girls were full of questions but Ima promised she would answer all of them at the breakfast table.

So Dena was alone. She had thought she would fall asleep the second her head hit the pillow, but she was lying here awake. Her head was so filled with thoughts she was afraid she might explode.

We're really back, she reassured herself over and over. *Everything is really okay.*

She wondered how long it would take for that reality to sink in.

Finally her eyes began to close. She saw visions of numbers floating before her. At first they all made sense and she could identify each equation. But then they began to get all jumbled and she drifted off to sleep.

Dovi on the other hand, fell asleep immediately. He had barely taken the time to wash his face. He threw himself across the bed on top of the blanket and within seconds, was out cold.

That's how Rafi found him when he entered a few minutes later. He shook his head fondly when he saw Dovi's sprawled form.

"Good to have you back, little brother," he murmured softly, climbing into his own bed. He felt a deep sense of contentment, despite his weariness. He had proven something to his parents, and more importantly, to himself. He lay down and within a few minutes he, too, was asleep.

Despite the fatigue pushing her eyelids down, Sarah couldn't go to sleep, not yet. She had to get Elisheva off to school. She usually walked with Dena but Dena was sleeping, and in any case there was too much snow.

Knowing that she was in no condition to drive, she made arrangements with a friend to have Elisheva picked up, promising that she would bring the girls home. Once Elisheva left, however, there was still Ahuva to deal with.

"Ima, come see my puppet show," Ahuva commanded. She was feeling much better. Her chubby cheeks had returned to their normal healthy glow, and her big green eyes had lost their feverish brightness.

"You know what, sweetie, Ima is a little tired. Why don't you make a puppet show for all your dolls and stuffed animals while Ima rests?" she suggested, hoping Ahuva would agree.

Ahuva thought about refusing this, but something about her mother's pale face and shadowed eyes convinced her that her Ima really did need some rest.

"You're not sick like I was, are you, Ima?" she asked, her face puckered up with concern.

"No, darling, just tired," Ima reassured her.

"Okay," Ahuva agreed, dragging an armload of dolls off the playroom shelf and arranging them on the floor.

Sarah thankfully lay down on the couch and closed her eyes, falling asleep to the childish rhythm of Ahuva's voice.

Chaim woke with a start, blinking in the bright sunlight streaming through the window. He glanced at the clock, and got up quickly with a little groan. He felt like he could easily have slept for several hours more.

The house was quiet. Chaim went down the hall and happened to glance into the boys' bedroom. He suddenly took a second look, his brain registering what his eyes had seen: an unmoving lump under Rafi's blanket.

"Rafi!" He called, entering the room, then more loudly, "Rafi!"

A tousled head peeked out from under the covers. "Abba?" Rafi asked, squinting without his glasses. "What time is it?"

"9:33!" Chaim exclaimed.

"I'm late for Shacharis!" Rafi yelped, springing out of bed.

"Be ready in five minutes, I'll take you to school," Chaim ordered. "Ima must be asleep."

Dovi woke up as Rafi was dashing out the door. He opened his eyes and stretched luxuriously, basking in the sunshine. All was right with the world this morning. He was back to normal and what a story he had to impress his friends!

He got out of bed and dressed, wincing slightly as he moved sore muscles. He felt ravenously hungry. He washed his hands and ran downstairs just in time to see the front door close behind Rafi and his father.

Ima met him in the kitchen, looking sleepy and bleary-eyed.

"I guess we're all dragging a bit today, huh?" Ima asked, stifling a yawn and smiling at him.

"Guess so," he agreed, smiling back. He sat, waiting. A funny feeling squirmed in his stomach. He had done wrong yesterday. He knew that no one had really addressed it earlier because they were too tired, but now … He wished Ima would scold him and get it over with.

But Ima gave no sign that she was ready to deal with that issue. She washed and opened a siddur to say morning *brachos*. With a small sigh, Dovi followed suit.

"Is Abba ready for his demonstration?" he asked over a bowl of cheerios and milk.

"Abba pushed it off until tomorrow," Ima informed him cheerfully. "He'll have plenty of time to get ready."

"At least he knows it works, and he has plenty of witnesses," Dovi offered, hoping for a reaction, but Ima merely nodded, and changed the subject as Dena entered the kitchen, still rubbing sleep from her eyes.

"How soon can you two be ready to go to school?" she asked in a businesslike tone. "It's already almost ten. In two hours I need to drop Ahuva off at Aunt Rivkie's house and go teach."

"Oh, we can be ready way before then," Dena assured her mother, and Dovi nodded in agreement.

Dena was neatly dressed in her school uniform, her hair brushed and gathered into a long brown ponytail. She looked just as she always had, except something was different. There was a wariness about her that told Dovi that she too was on edge, waiting to face the consequences of their little escapade.

Suddenly Dovi was eager to go to school, to escape the tension, the waiting, the pretending that nothing had happened. He got up and placed his bowl and spoon in the sink.

"I'm ready to go now," he said.

Ima raised her eyebrows in surprise. Usually she practically had to push Dovi out the door to get him to leave on time. Now he was volunteering to leave before he had to?

"Are you alright?" she asked him, not sure whether or not to be concerned.

"I'm not ready," Dena said, getting herself breakfast.

"Are you alright?" Ima asked her. Dena was usually the first who was ready to leave each morning.

"We're fine," the twins answered in one voice. That sounded more like them.

Abba and Rafi sat together at the dining room table, their heads bent forward over the notebook between them. Abba patiently went through each problem, explaining every step. Then he asked Rafi to repeat it and do a problem on his own.

Rafi was astonished to see that it all made sense. How had it seemed so incomprehensible just yesterday? But Abba had a way of explaining things, of making them seem so clear.

At last, they sat back, feeling closer to each other than they had in a while.

"I really think I understand this now," Rafi marveled appreciatively.

Abba smiled at his oldest son. They were alone in the house — no disruptions, no distractions.

"I think you do, too," he agreed. "You just need to believe in yourself the way I do. The way you believed in me," he added quietly.

Rafi looked up quickly at his father. The conversation had been very carefully steered away from last night's events but Rafi felt the need to discuss it, to process everything that had happened.

"Abba," he began. "I really am very sorry about what happened yesterday when I was supposed to be in charge. I don't know how I let that happen-"

"I do," Abba interrupted him. Rafi stared at his father, surprised. "Because you didn't let it happen. It happened, and the truth is, it could have happened if Ima was home or if I was home too. I was careless about leaving the door unlocked, about leaving the computer on … I was distracted and it made me careless. I'm the one who is responsible for what happened yesterday, not you." He held Rafi's eyes until he was sure the boy understood and accepted what he had said.

And the twins are responsible, he thought, but did not say. There would be time to ponder that later.

I thought I took all the necessary precautions to keep my family safe from my work. But the kids are growing up and my safeguards have to grow with them. I underestimated them and it must never happen again, Chaim thought to himself.

At his father's words Rafi felt a great weight slide off his shoulders. His father really didn't blame him, and he could feel the truth of the contention that this could have happened any time. He hadn't been neglectful or irresponsible. His father was not disappointed in him.

"I'm proud of what you did last night. Now, get to school and take that test," Abba ordered, smiling at him. "And Rafi," he called as Rafi shrugged into his coat and opened the front door, "just do your best. That'll be enough."

"ELISHEVA?" AHUVA VENTURED, cradling her baby doll in her arms possessively.

"Hmm?" Elisheva didn't look up from the tower she was carefully building by balancing one unsharpened pencil on top of another.

"Did we help?"

Now Elisheva did look up and her careful creation came tumbling down.

"No, I guess we didn't," she admitted, bending down to gather her pencils and begin again. "Sometimes grownups do figure stuff out on their own."

Ahuva gently brushed her doll's hair as she pondered that.

"I think Ima was a little angry that we tried to help," she confided.

Elisheva agreed with her little sister's assessment. She had been thinking and thinking about it and she couldn't understand what her mother had been all upset about. Okay, so the grown-ups had found the twins on their own, but still, their idea had been such a good one. It was a shame they hadn't really had the chance to try it. Before she had left for school that morning, Ima had made sure that she and Ahuva had cleaned up every crumb. Then she had given them a long lecture about wasting food.

But Elisheva still didn't understand what the big deal was.

"I guess Ima was upset 'cause we got out of bed without permission," she surmised. "But don't worry. Next time, we'll definitely be able to help!"

Chaim and Jeff worked together, quickly and efficiently. Words were limited to "hand me that cable please" or "do you remember the matter-energy ratio at conversion, stage three?"

They knew what they had to do and they did it, working to have the MEC up and running by tomorrow morning. The demonstration was scheduled for ten o'clock.

We'll be ready, Chaim thought, and he meant it. They had learned so much in the last thirty hours, and have solved more problems during that one night than they had in months previously.

How did it happen? he wondered. *How did we miss the answers for so long only to come up with them at crunch time?*

But he knew the answer to that. It was the twins. It was the pressing need to help them. It was a little girl innocently pressing some buttons on a keyboard after her brother thoughtlessly spun a few dials. He couldn't fail to see the *hashgachah pratis* in all that had occurred.

There was still work to be done, definitely. The technology was unsteady, barely functional, and so new. But they were finally on the right track. *If only I saw what to do about the twins so clearly,* Chaim thought wryly, grunting as he twisted the screwdriver, tightening the bolts on two metal rods. *On the one hand, they could have killed themselves. On the other hand, they provided answers we been searching for for ages. Do we punish them or commend them?*

"How are you coming with that?" Jeff's voice interrupted his thoughts.

"I've replaced just about every component in this thing, according to the new specifications we worked out," Chaim answered. "It's just about done. How about you?"

"I just finished entering the new programming. In small doses the machine should transfer matter to energy and store it, without blowing up. I hope," Jeff qualified with a wry chuckle. "In any case, it should be enough for a small demonstration, if we're careful. Oh, and our test material has to have its own energy source."

Chaim nodded. "Should we run some tests?"

Jeff groaned. "We probably should, but forgive me if I just can't face it. We've done all we could. It will either work or it won't. It's out of our control now."

Chaim agreed with his friend.

"You're right. G-d-willing, it'll go well."

"Yes. G-d-willing."

He paused, wanting to share with his friend the thoughts that had been running through his head.

"Last night was a night of miracles," he said finally. "The biggest miracle being that the twins survived, of course, but also, how everything came together when we needed it to, even though we didn't really know what we were doing. So much could have gone wrong and didn't." He shook his head, still marveling at the events he had witnessed.

"It's called Divine Providence," Chaim informed him, smiling gently at his friend's amazement. "Hashem made everything happen exactly as it was supposed to. And we'll always be grateful."

Jeff nodded, accepting the proof of his own eyes. G-d had definitely been with them that night. It warranted further thought. Maybe it was time to stop keeping G-d and science so separate in his own mind.

After another moment of quiet contemplation, Jeff headed for the door.

"I'll see you tomorrow at nine then, to get set up," Jeff said, putting on his coat. "Get some rest, my friend. We deserve it."

Rafi wrote steadily, working through each problem the way his father had showed him. His concentration narrowed to focus only on his paper, so he was startled when the teacher announced, "Ten minutes left."

He glanced quickly through his test. Ten minutes would give him just enough time to finish the last question and check his work.

As he handed in his test a few minutes later, Rafi stood with his chin up and his shoulders squared. He had done his best and he was confident that he had done well.

His friend Naftali was waiting for him outside the classroom.

"So what did you think? You think you passed?" Naftali asked, buttoning up his coat and preparing to face the snowy walk home.

Rafi smiled at his friend.

"Yeah," he replied. "Yeah, I think I did alright."

Naftali seemed taken aback by Rafi's calm demeanor. Just the other day, Rafi had been bemoaning his chances for his geometry midterm. He peered at Rafi curiously, but Rafi just continued to smile serenely.

"Well, I guess having a physicist for a father didn't hurt you any," Naftali muttered finally.

Rafi laughed gently at his friend's confusion.

"No, I guess it didn't hurt me any," he agreed, and then headed home to get some sleep. He still had some catching up to do.

Dovi sat at the table and fidgeted nervously, while Dena sat next to him, just as nervous, but tense and still. Their parents regarded them seriously. The dinner dishes had been cleared away; the table was empty. There were no distractions from their parents' gazes.

"So," Abba cleared his throat. "As far as Ima and I can tell, your time spent as energy didn't do you any permanent harm, *baruch Hashem*. We'll still want to have you both examined by a doctor, just to be sure. *And*, I want to make sure you realize that you can't tell anyone about this ... *ever*."

He paused, and both twins nodded their understanding.

"Now, about how you got into that mess in the first place," Abba continued, "I want to make something clear. All three of us are equally at fault."

"But —" Dovi tried to speak, but his father held up his hand to silence him.

"We were all careless, irresponsible, and negligent," Abba enumerated.

"Abba, it wasn't —" Dena spoke up, but again Abba waved for silence.

"We heard your story. You had your chance to speak, now it's my turn." He stared at them until he was sure there would be no more interruptions. "It's true that ultimately, your little adventure did me some good but that doesn't change the fact that you could have killed yourselves," Abba went on severely. He had to impress upon them this crucial point. "And that's aside from the terrible worry you caused everyone."

Ashamed, the twins studied the tablecloth. Dovi traced a senseless pattern with his fingertip, and Dena wrapped her arms around herself protectively.

"Dovi, when you saw I wasn't in the lab you should have left immediately, without touching anything. Because you caused me so much extra work, I think it's only fair that you make up for it by taking over all the housework that I would ordinarily do this week. That includes shoveling the driveway, sidewalks, and porch steps, and taking out the garbage. Do you understand?"

"Yes, Abba," Dovi answered meekly, not even daring to mention how this would take him away from his plans to build a snow fort with his friends.

"And Dena," Abba turned to her. "As soon as Dovi told you what he did, you should have refused to go with him to the basement until you spoke to me or Ima. You saw my project, you knew what it was about, I warned you that it was dangerous, but you ignored all that and decided to fix it yourself."

He paused and she nodded sadly. It was the biggest mistake she had ever made.

"Dovi told me about your 'deal,'" he told her. "You were so eager to get out of an obligation you considered unpleasant that you went against your better judgment and put yourself and your brother in jeopardy, as well as nearly destroying years of my work. You need to learn where your responsibilities lie and so, you're deal is off; you will sell all ten of your Tu B'Shvat fruit baskets yourself by the end of the week. Is that clear?"

She winced, but didn't argue.

Now Ima, silent until now, spoke up. "We want you to know, though, that we're very proud of how you handled the situation once you realized what had happened. You were smart, you faced your problems and found solutions, and you worked together." She smiled at them, and they perked up, feeling a little better.

"Now, does anyone have anything to add before we say goodnight?" Ima asked, glad the atmosphere had lightened.

Dena did. "Abba, Ima, would you like to buy a Tu B'Shvat fruit basket?"

CHAIM AND JEFF STOOD SIDE BY SIDE as the board members of Mark Technologies and their colleagues filed into the lab.

"We're ready to demonstrate the effectiveness the MEC on a small scale," Chaim announced when everyone was settled.

He took his place in front of the computer, and Jeff stood beside the MEC. It felt strange to see one of their usual technicians monitoring the readout screen instead of Officer Tendall.

On the stool in front of the MEC lay a nondescript piece of metal attached to several electrical wires.

"This is what we will transform," Chaim told his audience.

Then to Jeff, "Begin energy transfer."

They worked slowly and carefully; they couldn't allow any mistakes. Someone in the assembled crowd gasped as the metal began to shimmer. Someone else covered her ears at the high-pitched whine, but Chaim tried to tune all this out. His focus right now had to be on keeping the two sides of the equation equal, keeping everything in balance.

The metal piece disappeared and in unison, Chaim and Jeff shut down the energy flow immediately. There was a distinct smell of smoke, and the lights flickered, but that was all. Freezing vital components and providing layers and layers of insulation had worked. The MEC had been used, it had done its job, and it was still intact.

With a silent thanks to Hashem, Chaim turned to face those behind him. Their faces registered expressions ranging from moderately impressed to honest astonishment. Mr. Mark looked positively stunned.

"I don't understand!" he exclaimed. "Just two days ago you led us to believe you were nowhere near ready for a display of this kind."

Jeff's eyes met Chaim's for an instant. "Two days ago we weren't," Chaim confirmed. "But since that time we've had the breakthrough we were waiting for."

"It still only works on a small scale," Jeff added honestly. "Anything larger, anything without its own energy source, and the machine would destroy itself. There's still plenty to work out: containing that heat, preventing the computer wires from melting, maybe even controlling that noise. Improving on the MEC itself so it can contain and tolerate larger amounts of energy. But we can do it, if we're just allowed to continue working on it."

Heads were nodding around the room, and several small discussions broke out. Chaim and Jeff waited. After a few moments, Mr. Mark spoke up.

"It seems we're all in agreement," he said. "The MEC project should go forward to completion. The company will continue to fund this research."

He paused as there was a spontaneous cheer from the scientific element of the group, and then went on, "I must say, I'm impressed. When you asked to have the demonstration pushed off I was sure this project was doomed. I'm glad I was wrong. What you've accomplished here is remarkable. Congratulations," he said graciously, and shook their hands.

There were more handshakes all around, and more buzz of conversation. Several people came over to congratulate Chaim or ask questions, and he responded with only part of his attention.

We did it! he thought. *Baruch Hashem, we really did it. Thanks to the twins.* He gave a private smile. *But I don't need to tell them that; at least not for a long, long time.*

♦♦♦ ◆ ♦♦♦

"We can't let anyone know what happened to them," Chaim commented to Sarah as they sat alone at the kitchen table, sipping cups of coffee. "I know how hard it will be for them to keep a secret like this, but they must. Their futures could depend on it."

"I just told the doctor I wanted them to have a check-up. According to him, they're perfectly healthy," Sarah said, again feeling the relief she had experienced at hearing the doctor's words.

"Make sure the twins understand they can't talk about it. If people find out … Well, it's a first, humans being transformed into energy. I don't want the twins to become lab rats or something, or be exposed to a lot of publicity from the media or …." Chaim broke off, having a hard time putting his concerns into words.

"I understand," Sarah assured him. "It won't be easy for them to keep this secret, especially Dovi, but I'll warn them again."

Sarah was so happy to have things back to normal she would have agreed to almost anything. At the same time, she realized it wasn't just the twins who had to keep quiet. It was Rafi, Elisheva, Ahuva, Tendall … Though she figured no one would pay too much attention to what a seven-year-old or a four-year-old girl said.

"And Officer Tendall assured us that he wouldn't tell anyone what really happened here. Don't worry. There's no reason anyone should ever find out."

"Good," Chaim murmured in response to his wife's assurances, though he still had a vaguely worried look in his eyes. "Good."

Dovi perched on the edge of the chair in Dena's bedroom while she sat on Ahuva's bed.

"So, Abba's not losing funding after all," Dena commented.

"I heard. How are you doing selling fruit baskets?" Dovi inquired.

She grimaced in response. "Ima agreed to buy one and Aunt Rivkie said she would buy one. I still have to sell eight more. I guess I'll go out tomorrow." She shuddered expressively to indicate her feelings about her punishment.

"Do you think Abba would have gotten the funding if we hadn't done what we did?" she wondered, changing the subject.

Dovi shrugged. "It doesn't matter," he reminded her. "What we did was wrong and a good outcome doesn't change that."

Dena stared at him. "That doesn't sound like you."

"Maybe not," Dovi conceded. "But I realized a couple things from this whole experience. You're all like one way and I'm all like another and neither one of us has the right way."

"I like how I am, and I like you how you are," Dena protested defensively. "I don't want us to be any different."

"Thanks," Dovi said, but continued, trying to make his point. "But we're two opposite extremes. I think what we're supposed to learn from this is to meet somewhere in the middle, that's all. And that's more than enough philosophizing for me in one day. I still think it's such a waste that we can't talk about our experience. My friends would have thought it was so cool!" he said wistfully.

Dena laughed. "That sounds more like you." Then she turned serious. "I think I do understand what you're saying. But changing is scary. It's much easier when everything stays the same."

"More scary than spending a day and night as invisible beings?" Dovi kidded, and Dena had to smile.

"In a way," she admitted sheepishly.

Suddenly Dovi's eyes took on a familiar glint.

"Uh oh, what are you thinking of now?" Dena asked, preparing to be pulled into another of Dovi's wild schemes or adventures. She actually found herself excited to hear his newest idea.

Maybe changing won't be so hard after all, she thought. *Maybe I can just relax a bit and have fun for a change without feeling like I always have to be my brother's conscience.*

But her brother's answer surprised her. "Next year we'll be in sixth grade and we can participate in the middle schools' science fairs."

Dena waited impatiently for him to get to the point.

"So?" she prodded him finally.

"We're going to enter," Dovi told his sister, grinning. He leaned toward her and whispered conspiratorially, "And boy, do I have a great idea for a science project!"

EPILOGUE

SOMEWHERE ELSE, A TECHNICIAN in a government facility watching a monitor noticed a rapid spike in energy levels. He sat up sharply, dropping his pizza into the box on the floor beside him. What could cause a reading like this? In all his years working in this security branch of the government he had never seen anything to make him sit up and take notice like this.

In fact, as a technician during the night shift, he was generally pretty bored. Not that he minded that exactly. Jared wasn't very ambitious. He came in each evening, monitored the screens and sensors for eight hours, and went home. He kept himself awake by snacking, playing cards, and occasionally chatting on the phone with a couple of friends in a different time zone. Not a very exciting job, but it paid his rent.

Now, though, this was something worth noticing. The energy spike lasted a few minutes and then faded. Jared began checking his equipment, looking for a malfunction, but he found none. Suddenly he saw the energy spike again, in the same location.

Where was this? Some suburb of New York, he saw. A residential neighborhood. What could be going on there?

After a moment's hesitation, Jared picked up the telephone. His boss would want to hear about this. It definitely required some investigation.

Jared smiled to himself. Maybe he would even get a raise.

"Hello, Commander Cormack? Jared Solway here. Yes, I just wanted to let you know I picked up a very strange energy spike on one of the monitors. Where? In New York. No, not a lab or factory, a private residence. The energy signature isn't something I recognize. Whatever's going on there, sir, I'm not sure it's legit. You may want to check it out."

There was a pause and then a deep voice answered, "Thank you for the information, Mr. Solway."

And with a click, the line went dead.

◆◆◆   ◆   ◆◆◆

Another pair of eyes saw something important happen in the Abrams' lab that night. Eyes that were filled with greed and malice.

"There was some breakthrough there," the man murmured to himself, fine-tuning his own equipment. "A breakthrough I need to know about."

Whatever it was, he was determined to find out.

Whatever the cost.

GLOSSARY

All words are Hebrew unless otherwise indicated

Abba — Daddy

Aleph-beis — the Hebrew alphabet

B'ezras Hashem — with the Almighty's help

Brachos — blessings

Chas v'shalom — Heaven forbid

Daven (Yidd.) — pray

Frum (Yidd.) — religiously observant

Gam zu l'tovah — this, too, is for good

Gemara (Aram.) — the Talmud

Hashem — the Almighty

Hashgachah pratis — Divine providence

Hishtadlus — practical effort

Ima — Mommy

Minyan — quorum of ten adult Jewish males
   needed for public prayer

Morah — teacher

Neshamah — soul

Shabbos — the Sabbath

Shacharis — morning prayers

Shema — fundamental Jewish prayer that
   proclaims the unity of the Almighty

Siddur — prayer book

Tefillos — prayers

Tehillim — Psalms

Tichel (Yidd.) — kerchief

Tu B'Shvat — start of the new year for trees

Tzedakah — charity

Yom Tov — Jewish holiday